Arthur Gray Butler

Harold

A Drama in four acts and Other Poems

Arthur Gray Butler

Harold
A Drama in four acts and Other Poems

ISBN/EAN: 9783337342135

Printed in Europe, USA, Canada, Australia, Japan

Cover: Foto ©Andreas Hilbeck / pixelio.de

More available books at **www.hansebooks.com**

HAROLD

A DRAMA IN FOUR ACTS

And other Poems

BY

ARTHUR GRAY BUTLER

FELLOW AND TUTOR OF ORIEL COLLEGE, OXFORD

" There he lies, the noblest Torso in our gallery of English
kings."   PROFESSOR HALFORD VAUGHAN

London:

HENRY FROWDE, OXFORD WAREHOUSE
AMEN CORNER

OXFORD: 116 HIGH STREET

1892

PREFACE.

—◆◆—

OF the poems in this volume, 'Harold' was written, substantially, sixteen years ago, but withheld for various reasons. It is based on the well-known novel by the first Lord Lytton, to whom I gladly own an almost unlimited obligation. Of the minor poems, the 'Hodge' series, with the exception of the two last, are an attempt to represent the wants and wishes of the country-labourer in less-favoured districts; while those entitled 'Religio Academici' are submitted to the public with much hesitation, being so imperfect and tentative a treatment of a great subject.

Most of these minor poems have appeared from time to time in the *Spectator*, and are now reproduced by kind permission of the Editor.

CONTENTS.

HAROLD

DRAMATIS PERSONAE

EDWARD THE CONFESSOR, *King of England.*

HAROLD, *his Successor.*

GURTH *and* WOLNOTH, *brothers of Harold.*

HACO, *nephew of Harold.*

WILLIAM, *Duke of Normandy, and his Duchess.*

ODO, *Bishop of Bayeux, brother of William.*

DE GRAVILLE, FITZOSBORNE, TAILLEFER, *Knights at William's Court.*

ALRED, *Archbishop of York.*

AYLMER, *Abbot from Normandy.*

LANFRANC ; *and* HUGUES MAIGROT, *Monk.*

BERTIE, *a fool at William's Court.*

SIMON, *a Jew.*

EDITHA, *Queen of Edward, sister of Harold.*

GITHA, *her mother.*

EDITH, *cousin of Harold.*

ALDYTH, *wife of Harold, sister of Edwin and Morcar.*

HÉLOÏSE, *a Norman beauty.*

CÉCILE, *attendant on the Queen.*

    Bishops, Barons, Knights, Soldiers, Monks, and Nuns.

ACT I.

Scene I.

Githa *and* Edith (*room in Githa's house in London*).

Githa. What is that, Edith? What are you fondling there in your bosom?

Edith. It is my dove, lady, my poor dove. It was seated by its mate upon the thatch, when it was pounced on by a hawk and killed.

G. Tut, tut, child, you have always some favourite in misfortune.

E. And may I not grieve over it?

G. Nay, there are other things to grieve over: the King dying; England all divided and in confusion; Normans in every good post in Court and Church; and Wolnoth, my youngest and dearest boy, prisoner with Haco in Normandy! And Harold, oh, why did I ever urge him to go to Duke William's court? He is so bold and fearless, I should have checked him: but I bade him go, and now month after month passes, and he comes not back.

E. But he will come back again, dear lady, will he not?

G. Ah, you know not that Norman Court. Then I was blinded by my love for Wolnoth, and now I see clearly through my fears for Harold. But, child, do not call me lady! Call me, mother, as I have before now bidden you.

E. Ah, mother, mother (*embracing her*), and you do not think any harm will happen to Harold?

G. Who can tell, dear? Duke William is a bold bad man.

E. But he dare not—

G. Child, he dare do anything that is for his interest.

E. Dear mother, all may yet go well.

G. And I may twine flowers like these in the hair of my Harold's bride.

(*Doing it, as Edith kneels at her feet. Enter* ALRED, *Archbishop of York, unobserved.*)

Arch. Ah, poor child! And mine must be the hand to aim the blow. Mine! for the sake of England! (*Approaching.*) Daughter!

E. (*starting up*). My Father!

G. What news, Father, what news?

Arch. I have been sent for, Lady, to the King, who is dying.

G. But that is good news, Father. What say all the Norman crew of monks and shavelings who have preyed upon him so long?

Arch. His old English heart revives within him, as death draws nigh: and we have good hopes he may name Harold as his successor.

E. Harold!

Arch. Yes, daughter: but we must leave no stone unturned to work upon him: and there is one service you

may render. The Queen, your Godmother, the saintly
lady Editha, he has sent for her also.

Both. For her?

Arch. Even so! Penitence will have its perfect work :
and the thought of his neglected wife comes back to him
as the shades of death gather.

E. And I, Father, what can I do?

Arch. You must to the Queen, and persuade her—she
loves you well—to forget all past injuries and neglect,
and go at once to her husband. Once there, let her plead
the cause of her absent brother, and urge him to acknow-
ledge Harold as his successor.

G. And she will do it. Small affection has she left
for anything in this world ; but she loves Harold—he was
her playmate and her girlish idol—and she loves Edith
for his sake.

Arch. And I will be with the King, and prepare him.
You will do this, daughter?

G. Edith will do anything for the good of Harold.

E. Yes, for his good, but——I know not if he would
like this. You look pale, Father.

Arch. It is nothing. We must use earthly means. Our
enemies use them.

E. Well, Father, if you advise it! But I would
rather Harold should owe his throne to the people.
It is for them to give the crown of England, not the
King.

Arch. No doubt, my child! But it were dangerous to
let him name Duke William.

E. Well, then, I will go. You have always sought
Harold's good, Father. Give me your blessing.

Arch. God speed you, daughter! And you too (*to*

Githa) go with her and let a mother's authority supply what is wanting in her prayers. (*Exit Edith and Githa.*) She goes to lift Harold to a throne, and herself to— Well, the fairer lamb, the nobler sacrifice! And it is for Harold's good, and England's. And now to the King.

(*Exit.*

Scene II.

(*Room in palace of* Duke William *of Normandy. Enter* Haco.)

Haco. At length I have given him the slip, my faithful spy, who follows me like my shadow. But stop, lest he have left his eyes and ears behind him! This tapestry! Here might a man well hide. And this curtain! So! Safe for a time! Oh madness to have come to Normandy! to risk Harold's safety for a Wolnoth, the hope of England for a boy. And the hours fly on: and they will not let us go. Some fresh feast! Some tournament! Some feat of arms! They cannot part with us; they see their dear English friends so rarely. Oh, madness, madness! Could we but know the worst, and quarrel with them, and break away, though that were dangerous. The Duke is— But hark! he comes, and the Duchess, in deep converse! Soft, I will hide here. This tapestry shall do honest service for once.

(*Enter* Duke *and* Duchess *followed by* De Graville.)

Duke. Shows he yet any signs of yielding?
Duch. Not a whit! Adela calls him Harold the immoveable.
Duke. Immoveable indeed; impenetrable! inscrut-

able! He is undaunted by my power: indifferent to my splendour: contemptuous of my hinted threatenings.

Duch. And he wins thy very knights by his noble grace and valour. Taillefer sings of him as a paragon of chivalry.

Duke. Ha! he had better mind his pipings. I brook no rivals. What is to be done? I were loth—   •

Duch. I wish you would talk to Odo, William. He is very wise, and—

Duke. Can mould men, you would say, while I crush them. Good! Send Odo hither! Yet stay, wife, one banquet more! richer than all before! richer wine! richer viands! costlier apparel! Let Adela be decked in all her beauty, and seat her next to Harold. And then—

Duch. And then?

Duke. We will see, good wife, we will see. Ha, De Graville!   (*Exit Duchess: approach De Graville.*

Duke. Where is your prisoner?

De G. I were loth to be thought his gaoler, Sire. The valiant Earl is—

Duke. Our guest you would say. Aye, true! But mark me, De Graville, I hold you responsible for his safe keeping. And if he leave this Court alive without my leave, your head shall be for his.

De G. Why so, Sire?

Duke. Because I will, Sir Knight: and if the order comes to you to watch him yet more closely, you will obey. No more!   (*De Graville bows, and withdraws.*

Duke. His spell is everywhere, even on my trustiest knight. Nay, it is on myself also. And so—he must be mine.

(Enter Odo.)

Duke. Odo, this man baffles me ; I have wasted a king's ransom on him, and he is still—

Odo. Harold.

Duke. What then ?

O. A man who knows his own mind, and perhaps— yours also.

Duke (fiercely). No man shall know my mind, and live.

O. Does that include me, brother ?

Duke. Do not anger me ! I should add, except to serve me.

O. Well, then, you would have him your vassal, good ! But how ? As King of England ? Ha ! that would sound well—an English king vassal to a Norman Duke !

Duke. Peace ! Brother, I could strike you dead, were you not—

O. So devoted to serve you. Why, William, I merely seek to know your mind about this man : and you turn upon me, you, mine own familiar friend.

Duke. Proceed !

O. Well, then, you would have him out of your way in mounting to the throne of England. *(William assents.)* Brother, the Seine is deep.

Duke. No more ! I cannot.

O. Poison, then, is sure.

Duke. I tell you, I cannot : he is my guest. All Europe would arm against me.

O. Not so ! An accident ! An unlucky mushroom, or a cook's blunder, a shade too much of laurel-water in the sauce ! *(William shakes his head.)* Well, then, if he must live, he must live. But have you spoken plainly to him, and told him downright—Englishmen love downrightness—that he must live as your man, to do your will, to work for your glory? Have you—

Duke. I have hinted at this.

O. But you must tell him plainly. Leave hints to churchmen! Plainness is the tongue of princes. 'Veni, vidi, vici.' Give me power, and I would be plain and blunt as Cæsar.

Duke. And if he yield not then?

O. Then to prison with him! Every one has his terror. A mother for her child, a miser for his gold, a Jew for his skin, and an Englishman for his freedom.

Duke. Tut, he might break from prison, or my nobles arm to set him free.

O. Well then, the Philistines of Gath put out the mighty Samson's eyes. But you eye me?

Duke. Are you a Devil?

O. No, I am your brother.

Duke. When had a priest a heart, or a churchman any thought of honour? Pah!

O. Most honourable brother, I leave you to yourself, and to your honour. (*Going out: William stops him.*)

Duke. Nay, leave me not thus, I am not master of myself at times.

O. I did but speak of it as Epicurus of old, the wise master, of his chance confluence of atoms. 'Tis a strange world.

Duke. Well, supposing this chance confluence put before him, and he yield, what then? What pledge have I that he will keep his word?

O. Swear him!

Duke. How?

O. Swear him as your vassal, your man!

Duke. Oaths have been broken ere now.

O. Nay, but swear him upon the sacred relics and the ashes of the holy dead. And then let him break that oath if he dare.

Duke (after a pause). His oath! Good, I like the notion. Quick then, good brother! Bone and relic, holy coat and jewel, from shrine and sanctuary, have all in readiness! If I move him, he shall swear it this very hour, after the banquet. Yet stay, you will hide the relics, Odo, when he lays his hand on them?

O. I will. These English dogs love not the jewels of Holy Church.

Duke. Good! and Holy Church shall profit by it when we come to England.

O. Ah!

Duke. Abbeys, mitres, sees, cathedrals; all shall be hers, and more, more, more. 'Liberè recepisti, da liberè.' You know me, Odo. And meanwhile shall the guards be doubled, the drawbridge raised, and Harold's person safely guarded. So! (*Exit Duke.*

O. Sees, abbeys, mitres, and cathedrals, all
Given in one breath! He thinks me covetous,
My worthy brother, and he thinks right well.
Did all the world belong to Mother-Church,
All save one peak of icy Caucasus,
I'd sell my jewels, set my lands in pawn,
Go lifelong barefoot, sackcloth next my loins,
Limp in the public highways, beg for alms,
To win for heaven that outcast spot of earth,
And fit it for a Christian's sepulchre.
But to the work, in which the Saints vouchsafe me
Their heavenly succour! And now—for their bones!
(*Exit.*

Haco (*bursting from concealment*). Blind him, thou
  bloody priest, and thou his brother,
Prating of honour, but to do the deed
More darkly, deep in dungeons underground!
Harold the eye of England, blind his eyes!
Never! and yet—and yet it may be done:
Done, and the world, the good unthinking world,
Not know it till too late: then, when 'tis over,
Say with a sigh, it never should have been:
But done, 'tis done: and so, what follows after?
There is one way, one only way to save him.
Meet guile with guile, deceived use deceit!
Be truth in peace thy jewel, but in war
Leave truth at home, and carry counterfeits!
Or live by conscience whole, or not at all!
Yield middle ways to soft-tongued hypocrites!
So shall we, bettering our instruction, come
To escape these devils by the arts of hell,
Then shine once more the angel. But he comes!

(*Enter* HAROLD.)

Har. Dissimulation, feigning, and delay!
So runs the hour. He will not let me go.
And underneath his bland and catlike smile
Flashes anon a purpose. Ah! I fear,
I fear for England.
  Hac. (*advancing and putting his hands on his shoulder*).
                    With good reason, Harold!
  Har. What, Haco, pale as—
  Hac.   One who has been in hell,
And heard the fiends hold council.
  Har.   How?

Hac.   Here seated,
Seeking brief refuge from these tongues of Babel,
I overheard two men, who talked together:
They spoke of Harold.

Har. Well!

Hac.   And then one said,
Yon Harold were a marvellous proper man
To govern England. Then the other frowned.

Har. Frown? Well he might, yet frowning is no
    murder.

Hac. Then said the first again, 'If I were William,
Harold should not go hence, but with his word
To help King William to the throne of England.'

Har. Odo?

Hac. (*nodding assent*). Thereat the other smiled.

Har.   The Duke?

Hac. The Duke? It was the Devil. And then they spoke
Of arts, contrivance, threatening force and fraud,
Captivity that shakes the strongest will,
And darker yet—

Har.   A captive! See, I go,
This instant.   (*Noise without.*)

Hac.   Hark! It was the drawbridge rose:
And there! again! The great portcullis fell,
The guards are doubled. (*Rushes to the window.*) Stay!
    You seek more proof?
Let me try! (*Goes to the door: is stopped by guards,
    saying*, Back, back!) See you?

Har.   Ha! We are at bay. (*Drawing his sword.*)

Hac. Worse! we are prisoners! Nay, upon your life,
No force! You give them thus the chance they seek.

Har. Then all is lost. Lie there, dishonoured blade!
                    (*Throwing sword away.*)

Hac. Not lost, if you are wise. But listen to me!

Har. How mean you?

Hac.   If I fall in robbers' hands,
And they exact my promise, am I bound?

Har. Exact? Your promise?

Hac.   Say, some robber bade you
Butcher, a villain's part, the trusting lamb,
Stifle its bleatings with its mother's fleece;
Or in the night invade your sleeping guest
With death-concocted potion? Would you—

Har.   Do it?
I would die rather.

Hac.   But if on your life
Hung other lives? Would'st let this villain-knave,
A thief, a rogue, a cut-purse, take that life,
That precious, priceless, all-transcendent jewel,
Dearer to us than wealth of Solomon;
Not yours but all men's, when one single word,
A word, not act, compell'd not voluntary,
Would set thee free?

Har.   Would'st have me?

Hac.   See there yonder!
                    (*Taking him to a window.*)
See, there is England, more to you than friend,
Than father, mother, loved ones, more than all;
And on your arm in her distracted state
Hang all her hopes and fortunes. Split in parties,
Undone by faction, with a dying king,
An alien priesthood, and a hostile foe
Watching occasion! You her prop, her stay,
Your arm her only safety!

Har.   Gurth is there.

Hac. Watching the winds for Harold.

Har.   Edward lives.

Hac. And round his deathbed glower the Norman
   wolves,
Thirsting to lap our life-blood.

Har. Haco, stay!

Hac. And you, you would be caged in fastness here,
In a loathed dungeon, rendering England's moan,
Seeing yet held from helping.

Har.   Boy, your words
Goad past endurance.

Hac.   Seeing did I say?
Nay, steel your heart, and summon up all your blood
For yet more dread revealings! In your ear,
Nearer! Walls hear us. Yonder crafty priest,
Who has with all his brother's tiger-heart
Worse, serpent's cunning, spoke of blinding you.
Ha, blinded Samson, summoned to make sport
For jesting Philistines!

Har.   What did you say?
Haco, mine eyes!

Hac.   Your eyes! Nay yours no longer!
The purblind wretch whose seeing goes no farther
Than a mere handbreath, thus, the scorn of nature
That injures first, then mocks her injury,
Will be your envy soon.

Har.   Incredible!
The Duke! A soldier! Blind me! blind a guest,
A comrade! As there is a sun in heaven,
You mock me!

Hac.   As there is a depth in hell,
I mock you not.

Har. And William?

Hac.   The good Duke
Though at first scouting, played and dallied with it,
And dalliance with suggestion devil-born
Soon grows to be a devil.

Har.   Swear it to me!

Hac. I swear 't.

Har.   Not on your sword! It has a stain.

Hac. Then by yon bright and stainless sun in
    heaven,
By maiden's honour, childhood's innocence,
I swear it, Harold.

Har.   You would have me then—

Hac. Under compulsion, and for England's sake,
Do what no force of man, or fiend, would make you
Do for your own!

Har. Lie to them?

Hac.   Fight them, rather,
With their own weapons! Treachery is their food;
Well do they thrive on't.

Har.   'Tis the worse for them,
I cannot do it.

Hac. Cannot? Then we perish.

Har. A lie! 'Tis infamy.

Hac.   And to kill is murder
In innocent peace: but, oh, what hypocrite,
What made-up mask, what traitor to true virtue,
Dares brand him perjured, who, from native truth
Enforced to desperation, stoops to use
What arms despair may prompt him?

Har.   Say no more!
I must have time.

Hac.   Woe to you, if we perish!
Woe, if in obstinate romance of honour,
Clinging to names, unarmed with truth alone
'Gainst tyrants armed, unmatched in artifice,
You suffer lust and rapine sweep our shores,
Our maiden buds deflowered, and swinish feet
Trampling on innocence.

 Har. Leave me, Haco, leave me!

 Hac. Hist! who comes hither? Stand we here aside,
This corner! Wolnoth with his Dalilah!
Nothing prevents him passing; feeble flies
Through meshes slip that are a bar to lions.
Let us stand by, and hear him!

(*Enter* WOLNOTH *and* HÉLOÏSE.)

Héloïse. And so you are going, Wolnoth, back to
England! That hateful England, with its cold black
skies and colder hearts: going with Earl Harold.

 Wol. To England! Never! If my brother wishes, let
him go. I will stay here, with you, with love, with
Normandy.

 Hél. But he may force you from these arms. I have
only love to keep you.

 Wol. Which is stronger than all. Sweet Héloïse, I
will never leave you. And, between ourselves, my good
brother is likely to want all his strength to tear himself
away. The Duke has taken a strong attachment to him.
Ha, ha!

 Hél. Méchant!

 Wol. Charmante!

 Hél. Allons, aux plaisirs!

 Wol. Allons!

Sentinel. Qui va là?

Wol. Normandie!

Sent. Passe Normandie!

Wol. Belle Normandie! Allons! (*Exeunt.*

Har. Lost to shame! lost to me! lost to England!
O Wolnoth, my brother! my brother! for whom I came
here, in spite of warning: and thought to bring him back
to a mother's heart, to a country's service. And now
I find him, in a mistress' arms, corrupt, degenerate,
degraded!

Hac. And this was the device of Duke William.

Har. Aye, or his priest brother. But I will pay
them for it.

Hac. You will—

Har. Leave me! my brain is fire: my heart is stone:
Good spirits quit me. Go! I would be alone.

Hac. Farewell! 'Tis but a word, and you are free.
Life's but a farce; make it a tragedy,
And the world laughs; to act too fine spoils all.

(*Haco retires.*

Har. A word, and I am free. Yet what a word!
O Haco, friend, what degradation lies
Merely in uttering of that little word,
Which, like the false ensnaring usurer,
Sets free the body but to exact the more
The slavery of the mind. Wer't but to die,
Merely to die, and with some stroke of fortune
Life-ending, brief, on the red battle-field,
Pass like an earthquake-shock, and all be over,
It might be borne. But blinded to live on,
Poring for ever into sightless gloom,
With blank dark eyeballs! and in that eclipse

c

Deeper than night, darker than Erebus,
Still read, read ever in the haunted brain
England's great agony : her slaughtered hosts,
Her flaming homes, her desolated plains;
And, worse for those who live than those who die,
The shrieks of mothers, ere their sons be cold,
Rapt in the arms of Norman conquerors,
Yet powerless to avenge them! 'Tis too much.
Ask what he will, I'll swear it; yield up all :
Truth is for men; with devils there's no law.

(*Enter* DUKE WILLIAM.)

Duke. Harold!

Har. (*aside*). Already !

Duke. You are weary of this life ?

Har. I am. Suffer me to depart. There is small
pleasure in a weary guest.

Duke. A guest, Sir Earl ?

Har. Yes, Sir Duke, am I a prisoner ?

Duke. No! nor yet a guest, unless I will it. You were
the Count Guy's prisoner, and I ransomed you, and so—

Har. So I should be your slave. In England we had
hung Count Guy for making captive of a shipwrecked
traveller.

Duke. Hang him, for the chance afforded me of
obliging so noble a—friend ! Nay, we wander from the
point. Let us return to it. You would depart?

Har. I would. My presence is much needed in England.

Duke. Needed ? and why?

Har. The king is dying.

Duke. And they need you to settle the succession.
Good ! It is of this I would speak. And now let me sit
beside you, as a friend, Harold. Give me your hand, and

listen! Twenty years ago, when I was young, when I dreamt with youth's ardour of love and of ambition, I sate one day thus beside your royal Edward. He was of other mould than I, meek, timid, retiring. Heaven meant him for the cloister. And then at last turning to me his saintly face, he sighed and said, O William, pity me, pity me! This Crown of England is too heavy for me. O evil greatness! O weary power! And then I answered in a merry vein, evil it is indeed, a very rare evil: would I had more of it! Well, we talked on, and on. He groaned, and I comforted. He spake of unruly subjects, and I offered him my aid to conquer them, until at last he promised me, when Heaven should send him release, he promised me the Crown of England. But you start; you withdraw your hand.

Har. It was involuntary. Proceed!

Duke. Well then, since that time, my wife—Oh, Harold. the pride, the ambition of these women!—my wife has given me no rest, ever reminding me of that sovereign end. And she has in her veins the blood of Alfred, so that a child of ours might without dishonour sit upon England's throne. But you are silent.

Har. I do but wait to hear what you would say, Proceed!

Duke. Well then, as on Edward's death the throne is vacant, and as England now needs a strong ruler, and—and as, in short, I am strong—Well! what have you to say to this, Harold?

Har. Nothing!

Duke. God's splendour, nothing?

Har. No, Duke William, I would hear what you have to say of it.

Duke. Say of it ! Why this, man ! I would be king of England, after the saintly Edward's death—whom God watch over and preserve !— and I would have you help me to it.

Har. Me ! .

Duke. Yes, you, Sir Earl ! Who is there with power in England like yours ?

Har. And you would have me—

Duke. Help me to the throne ! When on it, trust me to keep it !

Har. Duke. William, it is the people of England who can alone bestow the Crown of England.

Duke. And the people are silly sheep, who run where the sheep-dog drives them. You are the people of England.

Har. This, then, I will do. When the Witan assembles, I will state your claims fairly and friendly, and leave it to their decision. Will this content you ?

Duke. Content me ! Let the minnows decide if the whale shall swallow them ? Am I a fool ?

Har. But I will press your claims. All that you have now said shall be laid before them openly and honestly.

Duke. And what if they choose not me, but take thee, man ? Rumour says you are ambitious. Ha, Sir Earl ! I have touched you there.

Har. Nay! In that case, if they chose me, I would refuse.

Duke. Till farther asking. Tush, we waste time. You are the voice, the arm, the head of England. What you will, she wills. And you shall make me your King.

Har. And if not, Sir Duke ?

Duke. And if not, you were better— Nay, Harold, anger me not, I would not for the world threaten you.

Har. You were better, you would say, beware: for Normandy has dungeons deep enough, and dark enough, for one who disputes Duke William's will.

Duke. I spoke not of imprisonment.

Har. And even if seeing men may escape from prison, yet blinded men, robbed of their eyes, are secure for ever. Eh! Methinks you look pale, my Lord Duke.

Duke. (aside) Treason! treachery! now more than ever must he be mine. What, sirrah, you doubt my honour? (*Harold rises.*) Sit down!

Har. It was but a jest. (*Continuing his walk.*)

Duke. A very evil jest! (*Rising angrily.*)

Har. And dangerous withal! One moment, Duke! (*Walks up and down: the Duke watching him: Harold gazes on England: then returns.*)

Duke. Well, you have decided?

Har. It is a great thing to be King of England.

Duke. And a king has great power to reward those who serve him. Listen! Help me to the throne, and you shall be my greatest subject. Wealth, lands, titles, all that a man can wish for, all this will I give thee.

Har. All that a man can wish for! All this you will give me?

Duke. And Adela, my youngest and fairest daughter, she shall be your bride, and then who so high, so great, so favoured in all the realm as Harold? What, man! still hesitate? Nay then—

Har. Duke William, I am convinced. Be it as you will!

Duke. In good time, Harold: for I was about to forget myself. And now embrace me, dear friend and future son-in-law, and then make ready for the banquet. See, Odo comes to summon us.

(Enter Odo.)

Har. (aside, wiping his face). The Judas kiss! O Haco, was it well? was it well? Done, done, done! I who would have died a thousand deaths sooner than utter one lie. But—Edith! England!   *(Exit.*

Odo. Has he consented?

Duke. Yes. It is done.

O. The saints be thanked for it!

Duke. Is all ready? Ere he have time to think? Ere he grow cool?

O. All! Bone and relic, martyr and saint, from crypt and shrine, all are there. They wait for Harold.

Duke. He shall swear on them before them all.

O. And then he is thine, body and soul.

Duke. But let the guards be ready, if he refuse.

O. For what?

Duke. To the dungeon with him! to rot in chains!

O. They shall be ready. But fear not. The saints fight for us. He will not refuse.

Duke. Then he is mine, and so is England.   *(Exeunt.*

SCENE III.

(Banquet Hall, DUCHESS, ADELA, NOBLES, FOOL.)

Taillefer (sings).

> Roses overarch the place:
>   Myrtles twine about her door:
> But a cloud is on her face
>   Sighing, crying, Nevermore!
> Will he never come again,
> Loved so fondly, but in vain?

Vassals at his bidding wait,
  Seated in his Northern hall;
But he frets amid his state;
  Lo! he starts, he hears her call;
'Galleys swift fly o'er the sea!
Southern maid, I come to thee.'

Twine the leaf, and twine the flower,
  Bridal wreath from orange-grove!
Sweetest crown of sweetest hour,
  Emblem of unfading love.
Waft him, O thou Northern wind!
Skies and waters both be kind!

All the North is in his might,
  All the South is in her charms;
Fairest Lady, noblest Knight,
  See him rushing to her arms!
He the Norseman, bold and free,
She the flower of Italy!

Duch. Thanks, noble Taillefer! You bards are ever sighing after Italy. Have we then no flowers fair enough in this northern clime? And now, my Lords (as the Duke still lingers), I pray you to excuse him. He has business of great import; but he will be here anon.

Fool. And when he comes, Lady, will he eat?

Duch. No, sirrah, the banquet has gone too far. No time for eating now!

F. Not eat! Then thank heaven I am no Duke, but a fool. Tell me now, gentles, which is wiser, he who has more than enough, yet wishes more, or he who has nothing, but is content?

Lord. He who has more than enough, yet wishes more.

F. Nay, he is a fool, for he enjoys nothing.

L. Well then, the other is wiser.

F. Nay, he too is a fool, for he has nothing to enjoy.

L. Both then are fools?

F. Aye, so! Discontent is a soaring butterfly that was eaten by a sparrow in the air.

L. And content—

F. Is a blind beetle that fed on dung.

Duch. Who then is wise?

F. God's splendour, I cannot tell. It was prophesied to me at my birth I should one day be jester to a king.

> If a man have enough, tho' it be but rough,
> He's a fool to seek for more:
> But as many as lack for the belly or back
> Are wise to add to their store.

1 will go and buy sword and spear, and conquer me an estate in England. Ha, Sir Wolnoth! what say you?

Wol. I am content here in Normandy.

F. You are a wise man, Wolnoth. Take my cap and bells!

Wol. Peace, fool, in England you would be whipped.

F. Ah, they never laugh there, do they, save i' the madhouse? But what is this?

(Enter Monks bearing a chest, with relics: guests all rise: great uneasiness. Bertie goes and lifts the cloth.)

F. Ugh! *(retires).*

Adela. Mother, what is it?

Duch. I know not, child. By whose orders bring you this chest?

Monk. By order of the noble prelate, Count Odo.

Duch. Some ceremony, doubtless. Let not this check your merriment, noble Sirs. What is it, Bertie?

F. A most uncomfortable, unsavoury aftercourse for a feast ! Ugh !

Monk. Peace, mocker !

Adela. Oh, mother ! It concerns Harold !

Duch. Be calm, child. But see, the Duke !

(*Enter* WILLIAM *and* ODO.)

Duke. My Lords, I have been delayed. But my time has not been spent in vain. Know all of you, that Harold has promised me his aid on Edward's death to mount the throne of England : and he even now waits our summons to this assembly, where he shall ratify his promise by an oath. Go, Fitzosborne ; go, De Tancarville ; and conduct the noble Earl hither, that the binding words may be uttered in the presence of you all.

(*Exeunt Fitzosborne and De Tancarville.*

And now, gather round yon sacred chest ! In it are the bones of saints, and the relics of martyrs. By that holy gathering shall he swear.

(*Enter* HAROLD *and* HACO, *escorted.*)

Haco (*aside to Harold*). Shrink not ! It is for the sake of England. (*Delay on the part of Harold.*)

Duke. Approach, Harold, and before this assembly of what is noblest in Normandy, I summon thee to confirm thy promise made to me by an oath, to aid me to the throne of England on the death of Edward, and to marry my daughter Adela, when the time shall come. Advance, Odo, and repeat to the noble Earl the form by which he shall take the oath.

Odo. Thou wilt swear to fulfil this promise if thou live, and God aid thee : and in witness of that oath wilt lay thy hand on this reliquary and swear.

Har. If I live, and God aid me, it shall be done.

All. God aid him!

O. Lift up the cloth! (*Harold trembles to see contents of chest.*)

Duke. Well may you tremble, Harold. That oath is heard on high. The dead have heard it. The saints record it. Cover up again the holy relics.

Har. And now, Duke William, I will depart.

Duke. Thou shalt depart this night.

Har. Come, Haco, come, Wolnoth!

Duke. Stay! Haco may go with thee. I have no claim on him. But Wolnoth shall stay as surety for the faith of Harold.

Har. And this is your faith?

Duke. It is.

Har. It is not in our compact.

Duke. No, but it is its seal.

Har. Wolnoth, come hither!

Héloïse. You will not leave me. You promised.

Har. Over the seas have I come to bring you, Wolnoth, back to a mother's kiss. Mount your horse, and ride with me : for I will not return without you.

Wol. Nay, Harold, I cannot come.

Har. And wherefore?

Wol. Normandy is become my home, and all I love is here. 'Tis cruel to take me from it.

Har. And England, Wolnoth, is England nothing to you?

Wol. Why did you send me out of England when life is love, and love is life, and the heart is everything? Normandy is now my home, and I will stay in it.

Har. False, corrupt, degenerate, degraded!

Wol. Call me what you will, but I will not go with
you.

Har. (*looking fiercely round*). And which of you has
    done this? You, or you,
Statesman, or Churchman, with your devilish arts,
Duke-demon, or priest-pander? O my God!
This man my kin? My noble father's seed,
Child of sweet dreams! Farewell, no more my
    brother!
Go, and be happy in your Circe's arms!
Laugh while we groan! Your mother 'll hear your
    choice,
And weep, aye weep, yet weeping hide her tears,
For scorn that she hath borne thee. Haco, come!
Let us begone! And you, your pardon, Sirs!
Forgive our plainness! In our rough rude isle,
Seabound, and neighbour to the northern wind,
That freezes up our tongues' civility,
We have small skill to garnish noble phrase
To gloss ignoble action. But in England
There is one word far nearer to the truth
For him who snares the stranger as a wolf,
Than e'er ye dreamt of, ye in all your pride
Of Norman chivalry, and Norman honour.
                (*Rushes out with Haco.*)

  O. Shall he go free?

  Duke. Yes! No! Release! Detain him!
Nay, I must trust him. Yet, upon my word,
If this same northern wind blow oft in England, .
Beshrew me, we shall need warm covering there.
Pest! What a storm! Quick after him, De Graville.
All that he needs, food, treasure, ships, provide him,

To our last denier! For with his good aid,
Angels and saints on high his oath assisting,
I trust to sit upon the throne of England.

(Curtain falls.)

Scene IV.

(King's Ante-chamber in London. Norman Conspirators.)

a. Have you heard? The King has sent for the Archbishop of York.

β. For Alred?

a. Who hates the very name of Norman, and will undo
all that has been doing these last ten years.

β. And Father Aylmer? Is there no back-tooth of a
Saint, no miraculous toe, that he can produce or promise
to the silly King?

a. Not one! The King is dying; a Saxon fit has
come over him, and he must needs make his peace with
the Queen, and Alred.

γ. That means Harold, not William, king of England.

δ. And that means these hammer-fisted Saxons
knocking Normans over, as you would fell an ox. I
shall flee.

γ. Whither?

δ. To Normandy: to the protection of the great
Duke!

β. I cannot, I am owed moneys.

δ. Owed moneys? They will pay you in coin you like
not. These Saxons are like their own bulls, stupid and
slow, or mad. There is no measure in them.

β. Yet wait! Let us try once more if we cannot get
Aylmer to the King. Ten to one but he will invent

some new marvel, some eye-tooth of St. Aloysius, some scapula of St. Anthony, which will do the business.

α. Well, we can but try. I will see him, and he shall do his uttermost. But if we fail, then—

β. We flee.

γ. To Normandy?

All. Yes, yes! Agreed! to Normandy!

(*Enter from opposite sides two* Lords.)

1st Lord. Well met?

2nd Lord. What news?

1st Lord. We are sent for to the presence.

2nd Lord. And the vile crew of monks and greedy Normans?

1st Lord. Banished with Aylmer.

2nd Lord. Truly this is news :
Yet much I fear me 'tis a flickering lamp,
Whose goodly show of promise comes too late :
His days are numbered.

(*Enter* Physician *and* Attendant.)

Sir, how fares the King?

Phys. The King, Sir? Ill as heaven and earth can make him!

2nd Lord. As heaven and earth?

Phys. Aye, truly, for he longs
For death, to be an angel; and the wish
Doth bring heaven nearer : and for earth—God help
him!

1st Lord. Is he so ill then?

Phys. He hath that about him,
Dropsies, and agues, hot and cold relapses,
Fevers, and fluxes, peccant taints and humours,

That had he lives like hairs, and will to live them,
He could not live : but hark ! they call for cordials.
                                   (*Exit with attendant.*

   1st Lord.   Eugh ! The wise man ! I smile but shudder
    at him ;
Pray heaven, his fingers come not near my bones !
Enter, my Lords !

          (*Enter* LORDS *and* BISHOPS.)
          The King is near to death.
Who shall his heir be ?

   3rd Lord.   In the street without
Men talk of portents, prophecies, and wonders :
A fiery dragon hath bestrid the air,
A mule hath foaled, a snow-storm drizzled blood,
With ancient words of Merlin fear-remembered,
That, ' Sit a Saint on England's throne,
Then is fair England's fate undone.'

   1st Lord.   Small need of Merlin to foretell us danger,
Whose hearts ache with it !   Ha, my Lord of London,
What say you ?

   Bishop.   Two alone can govern England.

   1st Lord.   William, or Harold?   Say, for whom art
thou ?   (*A pause.*)   For Harold?

   Bishop.   He is wise and full of valour.

   1st Lord.   Or William ?

   Bishop.   He is wise, and valiant also.

   1st Lord.   He is a tyrant.

   Bishop.   Only if you thwart him.
That which you fear, his terrible ' I will,'
Once yours, will be your safeguard.   He will keep you
From waspish Welshman and marauding Dane,

Who, hemmed like winter to his howling seas,
Will till his wastes, not waste you. Ye shall be—
    1st Lord. Well-fed, well-guarded, like a muzzled bear,
Bid dance, if one pipe to him. Out upon it!
You choke me, Sir, you have a Norman tongue.
    Voices. The Norman, never!
    1st Lord. Then ye are for Harold?
    3rd Lord. All to one man, to live and die for Harold.
    1st Lord. Well said! Cry Harold, and defy the
      world!
We'll have him yet; but lo! the Archbishop coming!

(*Enter* ARCHBISHOP, *attended.*)

Your Grace is for the king?
    Arch.   In dying ears
To instil earth's latest duty.
    1st Lord.   To name Harold?
                        (*Archbishop assents.*)
Whisper it not! But cry it thunder-tongued,
Till the earth shake! Oh! give it voice enough,
Till heaven's wide undulations crack with sound!
Once sounded here all hearts shall echo it.
    Arch. I know my duty, Sir.
    1st Lord.   I know thou dost,
But am too fearful to be reverent.
Rude times breed rudeness. Go then, good Arch-
    bishop,
Thou bearest a nation's jewel in thy bosom;
Guard it, and flinch not. (*Exit Archbishop.*) There now
    goes a man
In whom the mitre has not chilled the blood,
Or quenched the warm heart, of an Englishman;

Would all were like him! Sirs, upon your swords,
You, noble prelates, witnessing our oath,
Swear none shall sit upon the throne but Harold.

Voices. We swear.

1st Lord.   Wait then without until the summons!
Now as one tired-out pilot quits the helm,
To find another for our battered realm!
'Mid stormy floods see England sink and rise,
Her own free master, or the Norman's prize!

(*Exeunt.*

Scene V.

(*Inner chamber.* King *and* Archbishop Alred.)

King. Absolve me, Father.

Arch.   No! Not yet! Not yet!

King. Wherefore not yet? I am a dying man.

Arch. Hast thou done all that fits a dying man?

King. What should I do?

Arch. Make peace, my son, with Heaven!

King. Have I not made it? Oh, not yet! not yet!
So many hostelries as I have built!
So many poor men fed with daily dole!
So many shrines! So many sanctuaries!
With masses said, and holiest anthems sung
By solemn priests, and white-robed choristers,
All for my soul! and yet—

Arch.   Too little all!
These are vain crutches for a dying man.

King. What, would you have me build more hospitals?
More couches for distempered tottering age,

New homes where children, fruit of guilty love,
Are tended by pure maids?

Arch. Nay, think of one,
More sick, my son, more ill at ease than all,
Now shortly to be orphaned by thy death!

King. Mine, Father! Mine! I never broke my vow.
I die a childless and a virgin King.

Arch. Aye, but thy country! Think of England!
Set
Thine house in order! Would'st thou turn to sleep
As careless servants, leaving wide the door,
Unwatched, unbarred, for robbery to creep in?

King. Father, my soul!

Arch. First lose thy soul to save it!
If thou wouldst win communion with the blest,
First must thou share their sufferings, weep their tears.

King. How can a parting soul heed things of earth?

Arch. How can a dying king seek peace in heaven,
Leaving earth discord?

King. Shrive me!

Arch. 'Twere unfaithful
To Him, who set me here His minister.

King. Hast thou no heart? Mortality in tears,
Crying, and contrite, crushed, and penitent,
Thou art not human not to pity it.

(*A pause: the Archbishop turns away.*)

King. Cold, not an atom yields; inexorable!
Yet has he that which I must have, or die—
Die with my sins about me. Cruel man,
What would'st thou have me?

Arch. So dispose thy kingdom,
As with the people, and the lords, consenting,

D

Shall make our enemies beyond the seas
Pause ere they come to conquest!

King.   Wilt thou not
Absolve me otherwise? (*Alred shakes his head.*) Send
   for the Witan!

Arch. They wait without. (*Despatches a servant.*)

King.   But whom to name my heir?
Hark, did you hear? -

Arch.   'Twas nothing.

King.   'Twas his voice,
The mighty Duke's. If thus he reach me here,
Will he not follow me to the gates of heaven,
And all the blessed souls keep far away,
So strong, so terrible? There with him for ever!
Who comes!

Arch.   The Queen, Sire!

(*Enter the* QUEEN, *with one attendant.*)

King.   Man is born to trouble.
Edith ↲

Queen. My Lord, your summons brought me hither.

King. Come nearer, wife, and kiss me: I am dying.

Q. Dear love, how changed!

King.   Best change, to change no farther!
Can you forgive me? Then, when all is known,
It will be known I loved thee.

Q.   There, above!

King. Where men are angels: but my kingdom,
   Edith?
O load too heavy for a child of heaven!
Who shall succeed me? The Archbishop here
Would have it, Harold.

Q.   Who so fit as he?
So brave, so noble, and so wise as Harold?
  King. Yet is he of earth, earthy.
  Q.   Nay, he founded
Great Waltham's Abbey.
  King.   And set over it,
Against all rule, authority, and order,
An abbot married.
  Q.   Yet is he so good,
The very child will quit his mother's skirt,
To come and play upon the knees of Harold
  King. All, all, against me!
  Arch.   Foes forget their feuds
And join at bidding of a word from Harold.
  King (irresolute). Domine, domine, in te, domine,
    speravi.
  Arch. He wanders. Quick! Recall him!
  Q.   Love, last night,
About the hour when leaden midnight tolls,
I had a dream.
  King.   A dream?
  Q.   And in a robe
Of splendour, with a more than monarch's mien,
I saw one like to Harold sitting throned.
  King. Came it but once?
  Q.   Thrice over, and a cry,
God save King Harold.
  King.   'Tis a sign. Thrice over!
  Q. Will you not name him, Edward?
  King.   Ye will have it.
  Attendant (enters). The Witan, Sire!
  King. Let them come in! (*Murmurs*) De profundis

ad te, Domine, clamavi. (*Tells his beads. Queen supports him.*)

Arch. My Lords, the King consenting to your wish, names Harold his kingdom's heir. (*Sensation, applause : cries of* 'We are saved from the Normans.')

(*Enter* AYLMER, *amid disgust of Nobles.*)

Ayl. How fares the saintly Edward?
King. Presently !
Ayl. Duke William sends thee greeting.
King. The great Duke !
Ayl. Prayers for thy parting soul go up to heaven
In every church and shrine in Normandy.
King. Said he, the Duke?
Voices. Begone ! No Normans here !
    (*Exit Aylmer wringing his hands : Conspirators seen at the door.*)
King. See, is he there? The Duke?
Arch. Nay, fear not, Sire?
King. But see !
Arch. The Father Aylmer hastes away ;
The people hoot him.
King. Safe, yet barely saved !
His master also would be king of England.
Voices. The Norman? Never·!
King. Ye will have it so,
But whether it be wise the time will show.
Or whether it were wiser to submit,
God knows. We are blind worms : our best of wisdom
Is oftenest folly.
A Noble. We will serve Harold well,
Even as you.

King. Me? Yes! You partly served me,
And more yourselves. Prop up the bolster! There!
And I have striven in gentle Christian ways,
Above the rude ways of this naughty world,
To lift you higher, to make you Christian men,
But failed : yes, failed. God would not have it so.
His times are not our times, nor His thoughts ours ;
Our years His moments, centuries His years ;
So need we patience in our vast desires—
For many stars must quench ere close of night,
And many lamps go out before the dawn ;
But it will come, the dawn. (*Falls back exhausted: Queen
and Archbishop revive him : then, holding up the Cross,*)
Arch. Pray for us, holy king, where you are going.
King. (*starting up with eyes fixed and staring*).
I saw them on the mountains, like to sheep,
Multitudes! Multitudes, with slaughtering wolves,
Scattered abroad, and none to shepherd them.
A Noble. Who, Sire?
King. Who, ask you? And the darkened sun
Went down in blood : and stars rose bloody-red :
And the moon blushed all blood : and earth beneath
Was white with dead men's bones : and lo! a cry,
A piercing cry that tingled up to heaven!
A Noble. From whom, Sire?
King. From whom? From you, my people, from
you! And a voice cried, Lamentation! Anguish! Moan!
Trouble to England! Trouble to England! Sanguelac!
Sanguelac! The lake of blood! the lake of blood! The
day of the Lord! terrible, terrible! Ah God, in mercy
save them! Blood, blood, blood! (*Tableau representing
the field of Hastings. Falls back dead. Curtain falls.*)

ACT II.

Scene I.

(Room in Harold's house in London. Gurth.)

Gurth. I do not like these plots : they savour more
Of Norman fineness than of English honour.
Yet Harold king, and England all united,
The rest runs easy : but—the way to it !
O'er thy sweet life, poor Edith ! Hark ! He comes.

(Enter Harold.)

Harold. To England false or to myself forsworn !
Rebel and traitor to the truth within,
Or to all truth, perjured and false for ever !

Gurth. Harold !

Har. Men die, yet sometimes from their graves
Peer up ill secrets like half-buried bones,
With some half-truth to blast our memories.

G. Peace, peace !

Har. What tyrant even in ancient times,
When men with heated pincers tore the flesh,
And racked the body, yet left free the mind,
Did ever such a poisoned draught prepare
For his worst enemy ?

G.   Alas, my brother !
O Norman fiend !

Har. Would I could meet him here!
Here with these naked and defenceless hands,
Reckless of vantage! he in proof, full-armed!
From his false heart I'd wring my promise back
And be myself again.
    G. (approaching). Nay, be thyself!
The holy Father hath absolved thine oath;
'Tis washed away.
    Har. Can he wash out the shame,
The inward loathing, the inveterate scorn,
The hatred and the horror of myself,
Which, like a stain of rust upon a sword,
Gnaws in my soul! Shall I not be once more
The man I was, whole, flawless, with no thought
To which the rude world might not enter in,
To spy out falsehood? Shall I start at shadows,
Fear eyes, dread whispers, shrink from slanderous
    tongues,
Brave to the world, aghast at solitude,
Things once I flouted like a tainted breath
To pass unheeding onward?
    G. Ah, for Edith!
    Har. Edith, what says she!
    G. That in this low world,
Where good and ill, so cross, so intermingle,
('Twould seem some Devil marred the plan divine),
That 'twixt the bramble and the precipice,
Goodness must often lose its life or fleece,
There are some deeds hard to distinguish; good
Not wholly, nor ill wholly.
             (*Edith heard calling,* 'Harold!')
    Har. Hark! her voice!

Edith (enters, singing).

In the merry, merry Spring, when the sweet birds do sing,
    And the young corn tips the furrow:
Then the dead earth breaks, and the dead heart wakes,
    And we bury the winter's sorrow.

Har. Bury it, aye, sweet soul, but deep, deep, deep,
Or it will out, like murder from its tomb.
E. (sings).

In the Autumn drear, when the leaves are sere,
    And the mist lies in the hollow,
Then we mount and ride by the yellow wood-side,
    In the track of the deer to follow.

Har. The song I taught her! Lo, my wound less
    bleeds;
Saint, thou art known by working miracles.

    (*Enter* MESSENGER, *announcing approach of the* WITAN.
      GURTH *speaks to* HAROLD.)

Har. (impatiently). Witan and Work anon!
G.   They bring with them
A crown.
Har.   And she a kingdom, and a life:
Edith!
E.   My love! But what? Thou art not well.
Har. 'Tis nothing.
E.   Nothing? Would 'twere some-
    thing! Once
I knew a maid, whose cheek was like the lily,
Drooping and pale, until she faded quite
And died of such a nothing: yet her word
Was always nothing: and she bade us write

Only, she died of nothing, on her tomb.
Thou art not well.
   Har. It is the time is sick,
And we, who on our shoulders bear its greatness,
Catch its infection.
   E. Let me share thy plague!
   Har. Enough for one to suffer!
   E. Then that one
Be me! I have in me a virgin strength,
Fresh, unexhausted, as a fountain's source
Feeding an ocean. Let me—
   Har. Let thee suffer?
My darkness cloud thee?
   E. Clouds rest not on me,
But on thy summits, where the eagles clang.
   Har. Those treacherous summits, where one fatal
   slip
May drag a soul to ruin!
   E. 'Tis thine oath.
   Har. It is my oath.
   E. And must thou bear the blame
Like some poor wretch, while he thy soiler lives
Happy and honoured?
   Har. 'Tis the way o' the world.
   E. It is the way o' the baser half of the world
To brand the victim not the criminal.
Think not upon them!
   Har. Think not? Then, not live!
Live without honour! Live, reproach of all!
   E. Nay, live until their venom choke itself;
'Tis in ourselves that we are honourable.
   Har. How in ourselves, knowing ourselves forsworn?

E. Sworn to dishonour, 'twere dishonour's crown
To keep that oath.

Har.   But break it for my gain,
Gaining a crown !

E.   Gaining a suffering load !

Har. The splendour seen, the load invisible !
Nay, love, thou knowest not: who in woman's form
Can know man's honour ?

E.   Not, as men have made it,
Distorted, false, and jangled, dialect ;
But of true honour, language of the skies,
We women know—

Har.   Thou art an angel, Edith.

G. Then as an angel hear her, and come back
To thought for us and England !

Har.   Give me time,
Give me more time ! Then, as the crowned oak,
Deep in whose bosom lies the thunderbolt,
A leafy monarch scarred with grief unseen,
I'll hide where I was riven.

E.   Wear thou this flower
For me !

Har.   Thy flower, thy jasmine !

E.   As it breathes
Sweetest in darkness, so true virtue shows
Most glorious in affliction. Fare thee well !

(*Enter a servant,* 'The Witan, Sire !')

Har. Let them come in !
They bring with them a crown to share with thee.

E. Oh, Harold, thou art all the crown I ask. (*Exit.*)

Har. Let in the Witan !

(*Enter* BISHOPS, LORDS, *and others bearing the Crown.*)

Gurth. See, they come to offer
The crown of England. (*Harold does not speak.*) Bid
    them welcome, Harold !

Har. (*murmuring*). His, his, not mine! or mine to
give it him !

G. Nay, England's to bestow on whom she will.

Har. (*recovering himself*). My Lords, ye are welcome.

Bishop. We are come, Earl Harold,
Prelate, peer, burgess, few presenting all,
To offer thee the crown, which thou hast long
As subject guarded ; nay, as votary rather,
As votary, who passing oft the shrine
Didst never raise unchastened lawless thought
Madly to covet its imperial gleam,
Nor gaze at save to worship. Now at last
Take it, 'tis —

Har.   Stay! ere yet the word once spoken
Fly past recall. I would be open with you.
Plain truth, plain dealing, I have ever loved ;
And now I hate all ways but openness.
Good prelates, lords, and worthy men of England,
Hear me a short sad tale! Come nearer, Gurth,
Let me lean on thee !

Lord.   Nay, we all have heard
Thy promise to the Norman.

Har.   Have ye heard
The oath ?

Lord. We have heard it.

Har.   All its horror ?

Lord.   All !

Citizen. And care not. 'Twas a trick unworthy him,
Not binding thee.

Lord.   And if it be a sin,
These church-made fetters let the church set free
With penance!

Har.   Nay, think not the horror haunts me!
I have been nursed in such a school of honour,
My simple word as English gentleman
Had held me firmer than a hundred oaths,
Sworn upon grinning skulls and reliquaries:
But others, but the people?

Lord.   With our lives
We answer for them.

Har.   Yet, there is a plan:
Sirs, stay a little. Ye have the Atheling with you;
Though young he may be guided. In him flows
The blood of Alfred. I will fight for him;
Whatever is of strength, or wit, in Harold,
Shall serve him as myself. I had rather be
Free, and not first, than foremost with a crown
Whose brightest gem was wanting. Sirs, what say ye?

Lord. At such a time no child can govern England.

All. None, none but Harold.

Har.   Yet the oath! Ye will not
Love me the less, that so I swore it, thinking
'Twas for your good?

Lord.   Love less? Nay, rather, more!
Which of us has not sometime broken oath
To lord, or lady? Never frown at me,
Sir Prelate! Would I had that field again
I gave you when—

Bishop.   Dear Sire, these noble fears

But bind thee to us closer, us to thee.

Har. Then, if ye be so willed to put this on me,
I take the crown. A people gives it me,
And for the people's good I keep and guard it ;
Ware he, who touches ! O narrow circle, yet
Girdling a world ! (*Takes it and puts it on his head.*)
    Light orb, it can be weighed ;
A hand can lift it, and its pressure leaves
No wrinkle save one moment's on the brow :
Yet on the heart its daily, hourly, load
Sits heavier than a mountain. Still, good Sirs,
Proud and most grateful for the love you bear me,
I take the crown. And now to bind up all
Into one heart : knit tighter resolution :
The coldness and the lingering heat of valour
Fan till it blaze : and in each English bosom
Raise such a wrath shall make men thrice themselves,
Valiant to cope with triple adversaries !
All must to arms : all, like the noble Roman,
Give up their best possession : for know this,
That ere our preparations have an end,
Each man a soldier, and our coast secure,
The Norman, long expecting such a time,
Will be upon us. Hence ! Each of you bears
The fate of England. Arm ! Unite ! Obey !
                    (*Applause. Exeunt, with Alred.*)
Go with them, Gurth ! (*Exit G.*) 'Tis done. The first
    step conquered,
The second follows : Edith, thou art mine !
O Love, whose bright illumination came,
Piercing, and turning all my gloom to gold,
How wilt thou, as a sunbeam at my side,

Bless every hour! But hush! 'tis Alred comes:
Once more, good Father!

(*Re-enter* ALRED.)

Arch.   Hail to thee, King Harold!
I have a plaint to thee.
Har.   Speak on, I pray you.
Of whom?
Arch.   Of one, who, at our borders posted,
Set in the fairest castle in this realm,
Sleeps at his post, and for a woman's smile
Abandons sovereign duty.
Har.   He shall rue it;
This ill-example in those highest placed
Creeps downward, and, infecting manhood's flower,
Breeds bitter fruit of wide incontinence.
What is his name?
Arch.   King Harold.
Har.   Who?
Arch.   Thyself.
Har.   What have I done?
Arch.   Hast thou not set thy heart
To wed thy cousin Edith?
Har.   If I have?
Arch.   Thou mayest not have her.   So the Church
    has ordered,
And the Church is—
Har.   The enemy of man!
Arch.   How?
Har.   O ye torturers, ye men of wiles,
Ye saints, ye would-be angels, making men,
Who may not climb your heights impracticable,

Splendid, but loveless, freezing solitudes,
Plunge into depths of devils! Hence, vain man,
Come not between me, and the maid I love!

Arch. Harold, is this a time to dream of love,
When England's foe stands threatening at our doors.
All through thine oath?

Har. It was against my will,
Mocker, thou knowest, against my will I swore it.

Arch. Yet never oath was more expressly spoken,
And never word more glaringly forsworn.

Har. Man without pity!

Arch. And is this a time,
When England weeps, that England's merry king,
Pleasure his law, a royal libertine,
Like Nero harping 'mid his Roman flames,
Should lie in love's lap, dreaming?

Har. Monk, thou pratest
Of that thou knowest not.

Arch. Know not!

Har. We are one,
One altogether, separate but in name;
Twin hands love-clasped, that move but with one will:
Twin hearts, like harpstrings, trembling to one tone:
Feet that in all the dusty ways o' the world
Step to one music: ears that hear one tune:
And in the shifting, various scenes of time
Twin eyes that see one picture. Yet this love
You would dissever?

Arch. Hard not to yield! and yet,
Yet I must do it. (*Aside.*) O Harold, O my king,
I thought thee one of earth's true noble ones,
In this untoward, this degenerate age,

A touchstone, and a very test of honour ;
Whom passion's blast, though shattering rocks beside,
Stirred not from its storm-beaten pedestal.
And now I find thee—
    Har.   What?
    Arch.   For a mere girl,
Lacking man's crown of virtue, fortitude,
Ready to fire the world !
    Har.   What wouldst thou have me ?
    Arch. Wed not thy cousin ! Fear the Church's ban !
    Har. And then ?
    Arch. ·   Unite all England, North and South,
Saxon and Dane, and Welshman—
    Har.   ·   By ?
    Arch.   A marriage !
    Har. With whom?
    Arch.   With Aldyth !
    Har.   Never ! Thou, a priest,
Counsel me thus? Thou, Truth's ambassador,
Bid me enmesh my still entangled spirit
With one more lie?
    Arch. What have I bid thee do?
    Har. To wed a woman whom I cannot love?
    Arch. To wed a duty, loftiest love of all !
    Har. To be the father of a hated race?
    Arch. To be a father to all Englishmen !
    Har. To sit beside a listless, loveless hearth?
    Arch. To make all hearths sing on, and joy for ever !
    Har. No more, I cannot. If it be a choice
'Twixt love and England—
              (*Enter* GURTH *and* HACO.)
    Gurth.   England shall come first.

Har. Gurth, brother, you!

G.   What Rome to Roman was,
More than the love of mother, wife, or maid,
That—Harold, it was you who taught us so,—
Should England be to noblest Englishmen.

Har. Words, words! Nay, any sacrifice, but this!

G. Harold, I love a maid, and ere yon moon,
Now crescent, orb into its perfect shield,
Trust to be wedded: but, at England's call,
I would forget her, banish her from my heart,
Divorce her memory utterly from my mind,
And there in that ungarnished room set up,
Once bright with all the flowers that fancy weaves,
No image save of duty.   .

Har.   And for ever
You could do this?

G.   For ever!

Haco.   What is ever
In this short life? Love's roses quickly fade:
Fame only lives.

Har.   But it is infamous
For fame to give up all that makes fame dear,
Truth to myself, and her.

Hac.   O Harold, friend,
Art thou so raised above all other men,
A head and shoulders taller than the world,
To sink into the flat, and common ooze,
With low earth-grovelling creatures?

Har.   Boy, you dream.

Hac. I dream: but dreamers in their darkness see
Things day-blind passion sees not. I was born
Of sorrow. Sorrow took me to herself,

E

Taught me her secrets, made me sorrow-wise;
And therefore joys that puddle happier souls
Leave mine eyes crystal.

Har.   And as cold withal:
Hearts dead to loving, though with eagle-eyes,
See only on the surface. Cease, I bid you.
This is my matter. To your station, Sirs!

(*Walks up and down in great excitement: they gather
    together.*)

G. You have angered him.

Hac. 'Tis a good sign.

Arch. How a good sign?

Hac. Had he said nothing, or smiled as he said, No,
I should have feared him : but he is angry : the truth is
with us. There is storm within.

G. This is cold comfort, Haco.

Arch. There will be interdicts, anathemas! The dead
will lie unburied. I will speak to him.

Hac. Stay!

Arch. In the name of holy Church.

Hac. And you will ruin all.

Arch. What then, in God's name, should I say?

Hac. Nothing! Let Edith speak to him!

Arch. Edith? The victim plead the sacrifice!

Hac. Let her say, Renounce me, give me up, and
we are safe. If not—

Arch. It is too dangerous.

Hac. It is the only way.

G. He is right, Father, he is right. Edith is Harold's
better self.

Hac. But you must see her, Gurth, not I. You can
feel for her loss. I can only—see ours.

(HAROLD *approaches.*)

G. Brother, I go.

Har.   Whither?

G.   To Edith.

Har.   Why?

G. To tell her of our trouble, and its cause.
Let her decide between us!

Har.   Her decision
Is made already.

G.   Thou wilt abide by it?

Har. As by my own.

G.   Farewell!

Har.   Thou wilt tell her?

G.   Truth.

Har. I trust thee. Go! and leave me all, I pray you.
I would be here alone, and with myself
Hold consultation. Friends, farewell; I thank you.

                         (*Exeunt Gurth, Haco, Alred.*

Har. (*approaching a velvet cushion on which lies the
     crown*).

Let the crown go! Too much I have adventured
For high ambition. What is 't to me worth
This gold, this dross, this paltry thing of metal,
Whose glare is borrowed from the false esteem
Of flatterers' eyes, if for it I must trample
The heart that loves me, and upon its wrack
Mount upward to a throne? I will not do it.
Already once my broken oath condemns me;
Will it not plunge me deeper, doubly-damned,
With my first act of royal greatness thus
To break another? and—for it was a woman,
Weak, lone, unchampioned, friendless but for me—

Laugh at her woes ? 'Kings' mantles cover all :
She was too fond : who recks a woman's pain,
Light pleasure's toy, forgot in grander cares?
Vows, honour, all, were nothing.' Perish rather !
If England need me, let her take my service
Free and unbound ! As slave I cannot serve her.
He is a king, whose will is all his own ;
And, where the heart is happy, is a throne.

> [*Throws down the crown, and exit.*

Scene II.

*(Room in Priory, in London, with Oratory attached : enter Nuns
singing* Alleluia dulce carmen ! *Behind them the* Queen *with*
Edith, *who stay, while Nuns enter Oratory.*)

Queen. Sweet music, worthier of the Courts above !
Is it not, Edith ?
   Edith. Sweet, and yet most sad !
   Q. Why sad ? they sing of bliss.
   E. But sing in sorrow
   Q. How ? If they ever grieved, their grief is old.
   E. Old, but the pain is young as Cupid's fire.
   Q. Hush, child !
   E. Some are there who have loved in vain,
Who pierced their maiden heart upon a thorn,
And still bleed inward : some who loved a dream,
And waking wept to find it but a dream :
And some who, gathered young in life's cool dawn,
Ere yet the swelling bosom knew its power,
Took cruel vows, and wedded brides of heaven,
Long ere hot noon repented. Ah, too late !
Too late, sweet sisters ! While ye sing of hope,

Straining to join on high the angelic choir,
As in some crystal fountain curdling up
Sad earth's foul stain, so from your heart of hearts
Wells up through hope's bright radiance dark despair.

   Q. Yet are they happy.

   E.   Hush!

   (*Nuns heard singing:*

        Miserere rex coelorum! Miserere miserorum!)

                     Is that happiness?

   Q. Stay! (*they sing:*

        Nemo potest cogitare,
        Quantum erit exultare,
        Tunc in coelis habitantem,
        Et cum angelis regnantem.)

With angels! Yes, 'tis happy.

   E.   But above!
What is't to us, cold, in the chilly night,
That distant gleam of morning far-away,
Not here! not now? That is not happiness.
The summer painted is not really summer:
And joy deferred to a too distant date
Is misery gilded over.

   Q.   Daughter, peace!

   E. Sweet lady, I have vexed you?

   Q.   Earth is naught,
'Tis very naught.

   E.   Not always did you think so,
Not in sweet youth.

   Q.   Yes, I was withered young.

   E. Not withered.

   Q.   Wooed, and wedded in my prime;
Then as a meteor from the firmament,

That dazzles for a moment, then 'tis gone,
Hurled into sudden depths of darkness down,
Spurned wife, scorned woman, and insulted queen.
    E. Alas! I grieve you with these memories.
    Q. Men are so hard.
    E.   So hard?
    Q.   Is it ambition
Spurs them? Then woman as an idle toy
Must be put by. Religion? 'She must yield.
Some newer fancy when our charms grow old!
Then, as spring-roses glittering o'er dead leaves,
Man's summer-heart runs wanton. All caprices,
All whims, all frailties, ever charged on woman,
Were first by man invented.
    E.   Is it so?
Yet I love Harold.
    Q.   Hush, it is forbidden.
    E. By cruel men.
    Q.   O sin to label thus
The will of heaven!
    E.   O greater sin to ban
What heaven has made so tender, so divine!
    Q. Is't so? Thou lovest him very dearly, Edith?
Yet though he be so dear, yet root him out!
    E. I cannot root him out, unless I root
My own heart also.
    Q.   Let that go as well!
Cut off the moiety of corrupted nature,
To save the other and diviner half!
Save thine own soul: it is an evil time.
Listen! (*Nuns sing:*

Quum revolvo moritura
Quid post mortem sim futura,
Terret me dies futura,
Quam expecto non secura.)

O awful in that hour, to be not sure!

  E.   Love is so sweet.

  Q.   But heaven is sweeter still.

  E.   What would you have me? (*gazing at sprig of jasmine in her hand*).

  Q.   Lay that jasmine down,
Sweet though it be, and breathing wedded joys,
Climbing about the lover's bedchamber:
Take up the lily! (*offering one*). Its calm lot be
    thine:
Soul of the woodlands, hid in virgin shades,
Companion to the lovelorn nightingale,
Fleeing the world for maiden innocence.
See, Edith, choose! Angels are listening near
To greet heaven's bride. (*A pause.*) Sweet child!

  E.   I cannot do it.
I may not do it: for my heart is Harold's:
And even on the awful altar-stair,
Breathing high vows, or bent in cloister pale,
Kneeling before the sinless Crucified,
'Twere Harold's still. And oh! what perjury,
What perjury though for immortal gain,
For million, million, years of joy in heaven,
To live on earth forsworn! No, Lady, no,
Ask me no more! The eagle has its sphere,
Above, self-poised, in brightness near the sun;
Let me, a lowlier linnet of the grove,

Cling to warm earth, and in a love-built nest
Thrill one true ear with music.

Q. Must it be?
O God, O God, I would have saved her. Go!
Bend thy proud heart! Be humble! Earth is naught.
Go to your oratory and pray! Yet stop,
Sweet Edith, hither! O wondrous beauty! Form
As of an angel! Eyes not made for tears:
Made but for love! I would have saved thee. Go!

(*Exit Edith to Oratory.*

(*Nuns sing:*

Miserere rex coelorum, &c.)

(*Enter* GURTH.)

Gurth. Where is she now?

Q. She prays.

G. She has need of it.
Poor Edith!

Q. Flesh and blood are strong in her.
Her nature, like the pebbles on the beach,
Shines not till it be watered, washed in tears.

G. Leave her to me! Her love for him is such,
That sooner than offend his path to honour,
She'll whet herself the sacrificial steel,
And win to Troy through maiden sacrifice.

(*Re-enter* EDITH.)

E. Gurth, you bring news, sad news.

G. How know you, Edith,
Ere I have spoken?

E. How? 'Tis in thy face,
Harold is—

G. Well!

E.   Yet something—

G.   Come with me!
Come to yon window! See, the wind is fair.

E. Fairest of all! It is the sweet, sweet South,
Which visiting young Summer, his fair bride,
Fills her with perfume.

G.   And it fills the sails
Of England's dreadest foe, whose legions dire
Cover the seas, awaiting but one word,
To break in tempest o'er us.

E.   Ruthless man!

G. And in all England lives there but one arm
That can withstand him. Dost thou know it, Edith?

E. Harold's!

G.   The king's! Yet has he sworn, alas!
By mouldering relic, and by fleshless bone,
From ghostly crypt, or solemn sanctuary,
Whose ancient awe lies heavy on men's souls,
To aid this man.

E.   I know it.

G.   And weak hearts
Think him for this accurst.

E.   And shrink to follow
Where he so gallantly would lead them on.

G. And then his love, start not! his love for thee,
Banned by the Church, is one more obstacle.

E. Our love, ah me! But stay; one question, Gurth.
He sent you here?

G.   He dreamt not I was coming,
Until I told him.

E.   And he spake of this—
This obstacle?

G.   The very hint of it
So moved him, shook his giant oaken strength,
I thought he would have fallen.

E. Noble Harold!

G. Thou art so rooted in him, so entwined,
Sooner than grieve thee, he would both together,
High-arching elm, and lowly-trellised vine,
Dashed by one earthquake o'er a precipice,
Plunged downward to the fall.

E.   Then I must save him.
But stay. What if we wed not? Speak, I pray you.
Have I not in me the same blood as Harold?
Speak, I can bear it.

G.   It were politic,
To reunite all parties in the kingdom,
Saxon and Dane, and show against the Norman
One bristling undivided front of war,
He wed another.

E.   Whom? Hide nothing! Whom?
Thôu dost not speak!

G.   I fear to grieve thee.

E.   Speak!

G. Aldyth!

E.   That woman with the cold grey eye?
Had you but named another, and not her!

G. I feared that it would vex you; yet she stands
Second to none in estimation, none
In wealth, war's needed sinews.'

E.   And you would
Sell him to her?

G.   She brings with her as dower
Rich Mercia's strength, with all Northumberland.

E. Mercia, her Mercia?

G.   Through her brothers' aid!

E. What is the surety for her promises?

G. Her interest!

E.   Not his? O gossamer bond,
Lighter than air! False viper double-tongued,
Slaying its shelterer! Love has nothing double,
Not even a heartache. Oh! but say, she loves him,
Him, not his throne, his not her interest;
And then, as Hagar in the wilderness,
I will go forth with my great grief alone,
Leaving her in his bosom; I the while,
Like Babylon amid her desert sands,
A ruined shrine of old idolatry.

                                             (*A pause.*)

You do not say she loves him?

G.   Speak no more!
We must—

   E.   She is not worthy of his love.

G. But she has power.

E.   O God, and what is love?
Is it not power?

G.   To hurt the thing you love;
Yes, it is power.

E.   Ungenerous, unlike Gurth!
There Haço spoke.

G.   And if she be not worthy,
The clearer will it be to all the world,
That Harold, loving Edith more than ever,
Loved England dearer.

E.   Oh, could I but die!
Die in this hour, beyond the reach of pain!

(Enter ALRED.*)*

Arch. Die not, but live, and live to pray for Harold!

E. My Father!

Arch.   May the blessed saints above,
Who suffered, and through suffering grew more strong,
Aid thy decision!

E.   My decision? No!
I have decided.

Arch.   Ah, so soon!

G.   But hear her!

E. Think not I doubt! When brothers say, Give up!
Women must yield. Could I have lived so long,
Loved by a man, the noblest of the world,
Yet learn from him no mastery? Could I bear,
When Harold suffered, to hear the hiss of scorn,
'All for a woman!' or when the vulture Care
Preyed upon England's heart, and victory fled
False to his standard, bear men's whispered groan,
'It was her fault! she was the guilty cause;
Another Helen!' And then—my heart would break.

G. Dear Edith! Noble woman!

E.   Better far
To break at once! break now! than hang for ever
A mill-stone round the neck of him I love,
A canker at the core of England's weal,
And, with them slowly dying, slowly die.

*(Falls at the Queen's feet: Gurth on one side, leaning on his sword:
the Archbishop with his Crozier on the other. Enter* HAROLD.*)*

Har. Edith, I come. But wherefore liest thou there,
Prone at men's feet? Look up! 'Tis Harold calls,
Harold no longer king but of thy love,
Look up, and say to all the powers of Rome,

Thou wilt be mine. No answer? Edith, love,
Speak! Have they told thee? Gurth?

    G.   I told her all
The hard, hard truth.

    Har.   False lie! You told not all,
Told not this oath. Hear me! I swear, if England
Woo me, with all her wealth, her power, her pride,
Its price thy love : its loss, the losing thee :
So help me heaven, I will not—

    E.   Swear not, Harold!
Thou must be king.

    Har.·   King, and let others choose—
The rabble choose, a priest their oracle,—
The lion's bride! I will be more than king:
Clad in the simple baldrick of an earl,
With thee beside me, I will teach the world
What 'tis to live. The name is not the thing,
Free life, with honour, only make the king.

    E. Thou must be king.

    Har?   And thou?

    E.   I will live on
To pray for thee!

    Har.   Thy husband?

    E.   Nay, far more!

    Har. What more?

    E.   My idol! I thy worshipper.

    Har. Worship! I ask not worship. Live for love!
My love!

    E.   I may not, if it ruin England.

    Har. And is this all?

    E.   Oh, break not treacherous heart!
It must be all.

Har.   Have I then given my heart,
To one so slight, inconstant, variable,
That at a mumming priest's first threatening word,
Whose monk-made canon thwarts the Eternal's law,
She casts me off, and scatters to all the winds
Vows that she swore everlasting?
     E.   Can it be?
Har. I thought her truer than her lightest word,
Fonder than oaths could make her, faithful still
Though not a vow told her fidelity;
And now I find her—
     E.   Is it come to this,   .
This, Harold?
Har. Wherefore did'st thou twine my heart,
So cunningly, I knew not 'twas entwined?
So sweetly, life seemed Eden? Did I smile,
Thy smile did echo mine: or speak, thou seemedst
Rapt on my words, all wonder, all attention:
Threw I the rein to fancy, thy light wit
Sudden as lightning, swifter than the spheres,
Would give my duller thought in brightness back,
Gold for mere silver. Was I melancholy,
Weighed down with coming greatness, thy sweet voice
Cooing as dove, and soft as midsummer,
Flute-like would charm my seated cares away,
Till very grief grew gladness. Yet all this,
This smile, this wit, this charm, this manner fond,
This melting kindness, all this sorcery,
Most exquisite, or else most execrable,
Was nothing in the world but woman's art;
Thou did'st not love me.
     E.   I not love thee, Harold!

Har. No!

E.   And must women die to prove their love?

Q. Brother, I have known love, and love to me
Has been no pastime, but the pain of years:
Yet loved I Edward less than Edith thee.

E. Nay, let me speak! Do you remember, Harold,
One evening—'twas a breathless Autumn eve,
The sun hung low, red o'er the burnished mere,
The winds slept, and the soughing reeds were still—
We stood beside a new-made sepulchre:
A soldier slept there, victim of our wars:
And you said, 'Happy are the brave who die
By England loved and honoured!' Those your words,
And they burnt in me: and, so lit in calm,
Such fires should be our guide in stress and storm.

Har. Edith, forgive!

E.   O dearest, noblest, best,
Who loves his country needs no love beyond,
No other bride save England. All his life
He toils for her: and she, she cheers him on
As he moves upward; suffers when he bleeds,
Bleeds when he suffers; triumphs now he wins;
Deep in her heart inscribes his victories:
And when he dies, her name upon his lips,
Each breath a blessing, each farewell a prayer,
Then Spartan-like she clasps him to her breast,
Proud in her grief, and by her hero's grave
Unfading keeps his memory fresh with tears.

Har. Dreams, these are dreams: you know not:
        Edith, love,
Recall those words! You know not what they mean:
You cannot live without me.

E.   Yet those words,
From you I learnt them.
  Har.   No, I said it not:
I could not say it. If it cast out love,
Life's necessary, pure, creative spring,
Source of all good, best nurse of noble deeds,
The very sacrifice may grow a sin,
Gift not to God, but demons.
    E.   Do not tempt me!
O Harold, be the wing to bear me up,
Not the arch-enemy to drag me down!
Hell lies beneath yon show of happiness.
  Har. Hell! it is heaven. Come! (*opening his arms*).
  E.   Whither?
  Har.   To thy bliss!
  E. Thy ruin!
  Har.   No! Who taught you joy was evil,
Sad misery the only path to heaven?
Trust me, it is more holy to love well,
Than in a cloister dream of holiness.
    E. What shall I do? He taught me; strung me up
To this high pitch, and now himself unstrung
He quarrels with the music he has made,
And breaks the strings of his own instrument.
  G. Brother!
  Har.   Not now!
  G.   Go then! and take thy will!
Let the king say, my people weep and mourn,
I will be merry-hearted.
    E.   Gurth! your words
Sting him to madness.
  G.   Not a heart in England,

But leapt more joyful hearing Harold king!
No eye in Europe but doth watch to learn
How Harold sways his sceptre! What? Thus changed!
False to thyself!

 E.   Forget me!

 Har.   And to marry
Another! Aldyth!

 A.   For the sake of England.

 E. Forget me!

 A.   No, forget not! Let her be
Thy saint, thy star, in love, in memory shrined,
A little lower than the angels, one
Who, more than woman, bids thee, more than man,
Live not for her, but all men,

 G.   Brother, see,
What choice is thine! Here fame, here honour
  calls;
Here England with an outstretched finger stands
Pointing thee upward. There the flowery path
Slopes downward, wanton: with it infamy,
Shame, and for wedding-march a nation's tears,
Ruin thine offspring, death thy progeny:
Choose! (*A short pause, then*)

 E. He has chosen.

 Har.   Edith! (*They embrace.*)

 G.   Brother, come!

 Har. Come life's long wane, and sad eclipse of all,
Dead hope, dead love, dead joy, dead everything!
       (*A trumpet heard.*)

 E. Dead! 'Tis not death, but new nativity.
Listen! It calls.

 Har.   Who calls?

     F

E. The trumpet's tongue,
Never indifferent to a soldier's ear.

G. Come!

Har. As a ghost, with thin and frozen blood!

E. Come as a sunburst on a sleeping world!

G. Come as a monarch with his armour on!
Let us be going!

Har. Whither?

G. Where thy people
Call for thy rallying presence. 'Norman wile
Works in our camp.

Har. I will expel it forth
With English truth.

G. Our merchants sigh for peace.

Har. Win it through war then, gallant Englishmen.

G. England alone is lost and leaderless.

Har. Follow, who love me! I will lead them on.

E. See, let me brace thy baldrick tighter up!

Har. Nay, now it needs not, I am braced up, all.
Within this girdle there is strength enough
To overflow, and in a thousand hearts
Beget the might, the thews of Hercules.
Ah, Edith, had we lived in happier times!

E. We had been happy.

Har. Wherefore do we live?

E. To help each other to self-sacrifice,
And teach the world through sorrow bravely borne.

(*Drum heard without: Soldiers enter slowly.*)

Har. Hark!

E. 'Tis the war-drum, glorious heart of war!
Each throb a nation's life, a hero's fame.

Forth to thy work! Come Norman or come Dane,
All will go well now Harold lives again.

    Har.   Farewell!

    G.   Come, brother!

    Har.   Life will have its way,
Though weary hearts be breaking every day.

    (*Soldiers gather round, and enclose Harold, who goes out
        with them. Edith falls upon her knees.*)

    E.   Gone! He is gone! Stay, Harold! But one word
Of parting! Oh, I have saved him, but at cost
Of my own life: a string snapped in my heart
Then, as he turned. O lips that were too harsh,
O words that should have tempered, not enraged,
The festering wound! I should have been more gentle,
Have soothed, not vexed him. Will he not come again?
Will he not let me word it o'er afresh
In language different? Once is too little;
Once! Should I tell it o'er a thousand times,
Never the same, and with a thousand tongues,
Something were left untold. He was so tender,
He would not let a ray of the sun strike on me:
And now, O night, night, night! Be not far from me,
My God, my Father! Trouble is nigh at hand;
Darkness, thick darkness, falls on every side,
And there is none to help me. Gone! Gone! Gone!

               (*Curtain falls. End of Second Act.*)

ACT III.

SCENE I.

(In the royal palace: enter the QUEEN *and attendant.)*

Qu. Would it were evening.
Cécile.   Evening?
Q.   Or to-morrow,
Or the day after, or, October past,
Would it were winter.
    C.   Winter is so cold.
    Q. Cold, girl! 'Tis nothing to the cold of men.
What have you there?
    C.   That little lock of hair—
    Q. By Edith sent him, as her best possession!
    C. An innocent offering!
    Q.   It shall cost him dear.
Ah, me! Can men who love not, learn to love?
    C. Aye, Madam, if we be but kind and fair.
    Q. Reach me that mirror! Fair? I am fair enough.
But who would know me kind as well as fair,
Must show me kindness first. 'Tis the weak slave
Tempts on the tyrant; and poor wives too tender
Make lukewarm lords grow cold.
    C.   Dare I to ask
Has he writ to you since he went away?
    Q. Too little to remember, or forget!

C. That is a pity.

Q. What is a pity?

C. That
He writes so little.

Q. All have had his ear
Save I.

C. His queen! Is that to share a throne?

Q. And oft as I approach him with request
Of gentler import, he or answers not,
Or sighs, or frets, or murmurs of his wars:
E'en in his sleep he mutters peace, and England.
I could bear better hate than negligence.

C. Were it not well he felt your power a little?

Q. My power? I would but bend, to bring him low,
As gardeners use to do some haughty bough,
With poisèd stones weighing its wildness down,
Till he grow gentle. Tell me, your great Duke,
Is he so great?

C. None greater in the world!

Q. Greater than Harold?

C. None, I mean, save him.

Q. And of his army, tell me!

C. I have seen it
At Harfleur, leagues on leagues of armèd men
Moving like dancers, every step in tune,
Slower or fast, according to the measure,
Till horrid war grew lovely with the grace
Of ordered execution.

Q. Ah, I fear.

(*Enter* AYLMER.)

Ayl. Fear? What is this? The Lady Aldyth sighing?
Has aught befallen?

Q.   I am sick of life.

Ayl.   Heartsick !

Q.   'Tis question which shall longer last
I, or my passion. It were well, methinks,
To die, then haunt him after.

Ayl.   Ah, what's here?
Some freak of fancy !

Q.   'Tis no fancy, Father,
I know what is, and is not ; I have fancied
A grief, like childhood's ogres, all the while
Knowing 'twas nothing. That was phantasy.

Ayl.   And now this grief?

Q.   Not grief, but agony !

Ayl.   What agony?

Q.   O dull, these men in cowls !
Whose eyes have flown into the bats and moles,
Apt to read missals, but in passion's page
Blind as Teiresias !

Ayl.   'Tis his absence grieves you.

Q. Worse ! 'Tis his presence, like a constant goad
Driving me mad : you know not jealousy.

Ayl.   The king, your husband?

Q.   And his minion, Edith !

Ayl.   That lock of hair?

Q.   Would it might strangle her !

Ayl.   Ah, that was wrong. Yet suffer one more
     question !
You sent those letters that we spoke about
To your two brothers?

Q.   Yes, they do not come.

Ayl.   Edwin and Morcar absent ! Excellent ! *(Aside.)*
Nay, that is well. We are commanded, Lady,

Not to waste pearls, which hidden ocean-deep,
(As thrifty nature buries what she loves)
Men risk their lives for: scattered numberless,
With all sea waste, sea wonders, on the shore,
What eye would mark their beauty? So it fares
With sated love: our coarser appetites,
Or let me say, our weaknesses of nature,
Need sometime purging; then, their surfeit over,
They crave what they have spurned.

    Q.   'Tis true.

    Ayl.   And love,
With summer-heat grown lax and negligent,
Needs stern-eyed coldness, like a nipping wind,
To make men heed what habit they put on.

    Q. Reason is good, yet am I sick of reason.

    Ayl. Lady, you sicken of your solitude.
I would prescribe you—

    Q.   Prythee, anything!
Bid me go stand in the teeth o' the raging wind
Uncloaked, unhooded: bid me on edge of flint
Stand bleeding, barefoot! bid me fast, kneel, pray,
Tell beads, give alms, with charitable hand,
Wash leprous sores, wherefrom the mother's eye
Turns backward loathing; aught to escape myself.

    Ayl. Nay, lady, I have kindlier work for you.
A little journey to Saint Edmund's shrine,
Where fifty Aves, fifty Paters, breathed
With unction, shall restore your happier mind.

    Q. I go. Worse cannot be. No change is evil
From these sad halls. Come, Cécile! Ah, my beads!
You have them?

    C.   Certes, Madam!

Ayl.   Allons donc !

(*To Cécile*) Her jealousy, remember, not her fears !
You understand. Be sage !   [*Exit Queen with Cécile.*

They are too late :
And the great Duke, when was he not in time?

(*Enter a Courier, in long cloak, disguised.*)

Ayl. Ah, François, the bienvenu, what news from
Normandy ?

Fr. The Duke has sailed. By now he should be in
England.

Ayl. Holy Mary ! Best of men ! best of messengers !
How came it ?

Fr. He was at St. Valery when I left ; the Duke, his
lords, his knights, a mighty army with them, the world
cannot equal it. Sacre ! You should have seen them
there, drawn up on the shore, waiting for the signal.
Then, tantara, tantara ! The trumpet sounds ! One,
two, three ! They are off. A rush, a race ! The devil
take the hindmost ! All on board in ten minutes ! Not
a scullion, not a drummer-boy left behind ! Then a hush,
you could hear your heart beat. Then, tantara again !
One, two, three ! Off they go, the last first, everyone in
his order ! And in ten minutes back they are in their
old places ; you could think they had never left them.
And there they were, all ready, only waiting for a
breeze.

Ayl. And then ? The Duke ?

Fr. Called to me, and said, ' François ! '—he knows
me—' see there is wind enough for a small shallop,
and the sea is calm. Take boat and hence to London.
Bid our friends be ready : I will dine with them at
Christmas.' .

Ayl. Well!

Fr. Well, I set sail. Not a ship of Harold's was on the water: the wind freshened from the south: the Duke will have sailed ere this, and then—

Ayl. Harold will be too late. And then, for Saxon write Norman over everything in England. What say you?

Fr. That I am hungry as a wolf.

Ayl. A la bonne heure! Come, François, thou shalt dine with me in the Chepe, and see these men careless and confident as ever. Allons!   *[Exeunt.*

Scene II.

*(English Coast, near Pevensey: Norman ships in harbour.
Enter* Fool.)

Fool. Ho! ho! ho! The fool first! Let the fool take possession of England! O brother fools! Oh welcome, land of fools! No goose has cackled, and no cat has mewed. And is this war? this letting of blood? and clashing of arms? Nay, by my sooth, 'tis a merry-making, a right beautiful and brotherly merry-making: and to see our dear friends, the English, we are come. Now to say, God be with you! Now to kiss them on either cheek! and hobnob over a flagon of ale! 'Tis a good drink, ale, though wine is better for the wit. Ho! ho! ho! I could think I was a school-boy playing truant. Who will pick black-berries? Who will play marbles? Who will rob a hen-roost? Sacre! How they will laugh in Normandy! Cock-a doodle doo! The jest of it! The frolic of it! But see, 'tis Fitzosborne.

(*Enter* FITZOSBORNE, DE GRAVILLE, *and knights.*)

Welcome, Sirs! Welcome! Make yourselves at home.
This is the fool's land. I bid you all welcome.

Fitz. How fare ye, friends?

De G. As eagles lately caged
Freed on the mountains.

Fitz. All the world your own!
Yet, are they mad, these dread and doughty English?
I thought that they would stand upon the beach,
As their forefathers did in Caesar's time,
And give us battle ere we reached their shore.
But all is hushed, peaceful and slumbering still:
Barely, while thousand warships throng the strand,
Yon frightened cliff gave forth one seabird's scream,
That now is slumbering, murmuring in its caves;
The very waves seem keeping holiday,
And round our prows in charmèd silence stand,
To see the imperial victor enter in.
So, Bishop, you did well to urge us on!

(*Enter* ODO.)

Odo. A miracle! a most clear miracle!
Said I not well, the saints are on our side?
Welcome to England, Norman conquerors!
Where is the Duke?

Fitz. Below us, on the beach,
Now on the land, now in the water, like
A sea-god! With a voice amid the din
Clear as a trumpet. Hark!

Duke. What! laggards! stay
Till England wake? Blow trumpets, sound a charge!

Horsemen and foot, quick, knights and archers all,
Into the waves! Fear nothing save my ire!
  A Voice. Who stays to guard the ships?
  Duke.   The deep, deep, sea!
  Voice. Why, Sire? This cuts us off from all the
    world.
  Duke. Because I will: your reason is, I will.
Out with them to the deep, and scuttle them!
                          (*Trumpets sound.*)
  Odo. He threatens, but with gladness in his tone,
Like some bright herald of a jubilee.
On, warriors of the Lord! on, Normandy!
I go to aid him.   (*Exit.*
  Fitz.   And we too. You, Sir, (*to an officer*)
Go search the country far as Pevensey!
  Off. We shall need stores.
  Fitz.   You have a storehouse ready.
England is a rich sponge, which being squeezed
Will furnish all, food, forage, provender.
  Off. If they resist?
  Fitz.   Then make a solitude!
Hang the ringleaders! Fire the villages!
Teach them their masters! Lessons writ in blood
Are easiest read. And yet remember also,
The Duke dislikes all violence.
  Fool.   Save, his own,
To kill a thousand, not a single man;
Blood in the gross, not driblets!
  Fitz.   Have a care!
Peace, fool! And thou, de Graville, send out
    scouts;
Nay, go thyself to explore the enemy.

They will not let us on to London march
Without one skirmish?

De G.   Nay, I know them well,
Like raw recruited soldiers, still unknown
War's swift surprises, careless, confident;
Brave, but unready! They'll be here anon.

Fitz. Yet see if there be not some treachery!
Yon Harold is adept in arts of war:
And haply this may prove some stratagem,
Which may the more confound us, off our guard:
Quick! Yet be wary! And, no violence!

Fool. And if thou meet a goose upon the way, De
,Graville, persuade him to come with thee. But no
violence! the Duke will have no violence! I would fain
know the savour of these geese of England.

[*Exit De Graville.*

Fitz. What say you now, Bertie? Was it a fool's
errand, this coming to England?

Fool. Yes, Fitzosborne, a very fool's errand; but these
English be greater fools than we.

Fitz. And what do you wish for now, Bertie?

Fool. An earldom at the least, friend, with a fat manor,
and a fairhaired Saxon for my bride. I have a flight of
heiresses in my eye.

Fitz. Good! but you must win her first. There is
much fighting to be done! Where are your cap and
bells?

Fool. Gone to the bottom! They were left on board!
Where a whole people are fools, your one fool lacks dis-
tinction.

Fitz. Fools indeed, beyond all extravagance of belief!
But now, go and get thy supper!

Fool. Supper? Should I, like Nebuchadnezzar, eat grass? Oh for a fat capon, and a stoup o' wine !

Fitz. Away ! [*Exit.*

Fool. Nay, I am well here. I will certainly marry here in England. My beef-eating father-in-law shall feed swine ; my mother-in-law spin hose ; my lady-wife make puddings for me. They be rare pudding-makers, these women of England. And I will teach her manners. Your islander is ever a babe in manners. To hold herself thus ! But fighting ? That great numskull, Fitzosborne, spoke of fighting for her. I like not fighting. Of what use to win half a kingdom in the wars, and leave half your limbs upon the field of battle. Can a leg eat, a head marry ? Bah ! Or with a spear in your midriff, like a skewer in a brisket of beef! Out upon it ! Ah, your man of words is your real man. When words shall replace blows, then shall your man-at-arms be fool, and your fool king. Heigho ! I would I had my supper ! But, hillo ! (*Enter soldier with pitcher.*) Whither ?

Soldier. To fetch water.

Fool. Water ! Rock of Moses ! And why water ?

Soldier. To drink, fool !

Fool. Drink water ! Is it come to this ? Oh war ! Alas for Normandy !

(*Enter* DUKE WILLIAM *and* ODO, *attended.*)

Duke. What man is he that sighs for Normandy ? You, Bertie ! You !

Fool. Oh ! (*Aside*) He has the knit in his brow. It were well not to vex him. I did but say, Sire, that a King's jester should drink wine.

Duke. Splendour of God, my knights, and nobles all,

Have we not here a richer, fairer, realm,
Than any we have left in Normandy?
Said I not well, yon channel was a ditch,
England a doughty, but unguarded, fortress,
Whose people, like their surly native dogs,
Fight, singly, bravely : but their hearts too fierce,
Too full of choler, rude, ungovernable,
To know obedience?   O Sirs, note it well!
Man's glory is obedience : sans obedience,
Which at the sounding of some petty pipe
Bids squadrons charge, their thunder shake the ground
Fire-breathing, like storm-wingèd elements;
Then of a sudden stop, as turned to stone,
Rider and steed like breathing monuments;
Numbers but crowd the shambles for our spears.
Ah, Lanfranc, see, the Church has a new realm!
But what is this?

   Lanf.   A banner, Sire, from Rome,
With which do thou, a second Caesar, ride,
Wider than Roman eagles ever flew,
O'er necks of enemies.   Go!   Be heaven thy helper!

   Duke (unfurling it). This only lacked.   And lo! upon
      yon mound,
Fronting the wild sea-breezes, shall arise
A massive shrine, like Zion, valour-won,
Then temple-crowned, to-morrow's lasting pile,
Our battle's mark, our triumph's monument.
See too these relics!   On these Harold swore
To make me king.   With these I will confront him.
What is this place?

   Fitzosborne. Senlac, or Sanglac, Sire.

   Duke. Blood-lake!   What prophet anciently inspired

Baptized it thus? We will confirm it soon.
But hark! who comes?

(*A scout rushes in followed by De Graville.*)

Scout. The English! The English!

(*Sensation. Voices,* 'Where are they? Are they near?')

Scout. Advancing with all speed against us, Earl
Harold at their head with his brothers; and an army at
his back of men as stout and strong as any in Christendom.

Duke. They come to their death.

Fitzosborne. Shall we not set our army in the field,
And make all ready?

Duke.   Nay. The sun is low:
They will entrench.

Lanf.   Then were it not well-counselled
To send, and twit the usurper with his oath?
His then the sin of bloodshed!

Duke.   Excellent!
See to it, Lanfranc! And yet one thing more.
Oft have I longed to measure swords with Harold.
Which of my knights will take my challenge-glove,
And dare him to the field? De Graville!

De G.   Sire!

Duke. Take this—

De G.   Nay, Sire!

Duke.   What?

De G.   While he lived for honour,
Honour I held it but to speak with him;
But with a perjured knight, a renegade,
Ask it not, Sire!

Duke.   I did not ask it, sirrah;
'Twas my commandment. Peste! You are too bold,

Proud, and punctilious as a woman. What?
I have your knee, your homage, your obeisance,
But—

    De G. Not my honour, Sire; that is my own.

    Duke. Proud spirit, peace! I will not hurt thine
      honour.

Tush, man, so shape and word it, as thou wilt!
Nay, must I vainly ask my trustiest knight
This slight poor service?

    De G.   Sire, I do thine asking. (*Goes slowly.*)

    Duke. What dares he not, who dares me? Tremble,
      Harold!

Hope not for victory over knights like mine!
Ha, Hugh, approach! What arrows have your men?

    Hugh. Each sixty, Sire!

    Duke.   And sixty more, remember,
Held in reserve! And, one more word, shoot high!
Then, when they look for mercy up to heaven,
Answer in arrow-flights! The needed stores—
Are they provided? Good! Let war feed war!
Yet one thing more! Do ye remember, all,
My turning movement, fleeing to draw on
Further pursuit?

    Fitz.   As at Val-ez-dunes, Sire?

    Duke. Aye, but the time! Mark! All depends on
      time.

Moments in peace are weak and valueless,
But moments are the hands of fate in war:
Better in peace waste centuries than in war
One priceless instant! Turn too soon, they gain
Their stronghold's refuge: turn too late, they catch
      you

In flagrant disarrangement. So, you take me?
Now, what remains?

   Odo.   'Tis Saint Callixtus eve :
Shall we not ask his blessing ere we sleep?

   Duke. Good Saint Callixtus! 'Tis my birthday also.
When I was born the stars were fortunate,
And their conjunction promised me a crown.
See to it, Odo!

   Odo (*going*). What is the word to-morrow?

   Duke (*after a pause*). God is our aid.

   Odo.   Yon sun goes fairly down.
To-morrow it will see a conquered land.

   Duke. Will, brother?—does! 'Twas conquer'd while
     they slept :
'Twas conquer'd when they left the unguarded waves,
And threw away like thriftless prodigals
Their one sole treasure, Nature's muniment,
Those sea walls, built of old by Titan hands,
And moated round with the inviolate sea,
The unfathom'd ocean. Lo! I set my foot
On England's pride ; nor ever England's strength,
Awaked too late, like Samson self-betrayed,
Shall make it budge. Their day of grace is over,
Our voyage is past, our step is on the shore :
Who lands in England is its conqueror.

SCENE III.

(A country village, near Hastings : old wives and girls spinning at their doors : other girls bringing apples from the orchard, young men helping them : children playing with the apples : boys playing single-stick : wounded soldier on crutch, watching them : all expecting the king.)

Scout (rushing in). They're coming : they're coming. The king, and his brothers, and the whole army. Close by ! There !

Farmer (bustling out of house). Mab, stop your spinning : wife, put by your wheel :
Girls, let those apples hang upon the tree :
Boys of all sorts, Hob, Will, and Harry, come,
Quick ! leave your games. The king is coming by :
I say the king, our Harold, with his men,
My son among them. Ha ! They'll be athirst ;
Fighting and marching make a soldier dry ;
When are they not dry ? Throats like furnaces !
Lips like a limekiln ! Go, fetch a hogshead ! Nay,
One, said I ?—two ; my cellar's oldest store,
Ale, cyder, both ! Oh, honour on the day,
That I should live to see his blessed face,
And he should this way come to guard our shores !
God save king Harold ! God defend the king !

(Enter HAROLD *and* GURTH, *attended, with soldiers.)*

Har. Thanks for your greeting friends and countrymen !
What ye would do for me and for my cause,
I know full well : and for my own true love,
Not to you only, but all Englishmen,
I would my heart lay open in my hand

That all might read it. For indeed I hold
A people's love far dearer than a throne;
And to be blessed in poor men's cottages,
Remembered o'er the bread they toiling eat,
Where bit by bit the store is gathered in,
A grace exceeding far the wealth of kings;
Not to be paid with pittance of poor gold,
Or meted dole, or scanted provender;
But to be answered like the gifts of heaven
With life-long reverent service. Therefore now,
Footsore, and weary many a fainting league,
The skies our roof, the stony earth our pillow,
Often in hunger, often, while we slept,
White-sheeted mists our only coverlet,
Cold canopy against the freezing stars,
We haste to drive the Norman from your shores.
Then welcome peace, when banished hateful war!
Welcome the farmer resting 'mid his sheaves,
The busy housewife singing at her wheel!
Welcome the youths' and maidens' merry glee,
Pressing for winter's mirth the orchard's store!
And save in mimic sport be war unknown,
A pastime gracing bloodless holidays!
Till then, till I can reign a king at peace,
I'll wear a soldier's armour. Give me now
Yon cup! I drink it, health to England's friends,
Death and confusion to her enemies!

(*Triumphant music, during which villagers approach with shouts,*
'Long live King Harold!' *Harold speaks kindly to them, reminding the soldier,* 'You-fought with me against the Welsh.
When that leg is well, come and see me at Westminster.' *To
a boy, who asks,* 'Was it this axe killed the giant Hardrada?'

he says, 'Aye, boy! when you are a man, so do you fight all England's enemies.' *Farmer heard, saying,* 'Drink this! That'll put the heart into you. That'll give an edge to your axes.' *Shouts of* 'Drink-hæl!' *Girls bring wreaths of flowers, when enter a villager, crying,* 'The Normans! the Normans! over yon hill! they are come!' *Great confusion, with cries of* 'Save us! Save us!')

Har. Peace with these fears! Am I not with you
  still?
Are there not here twice twenty thousand men,
Who crushed the Dane, and vanquished Hardrada?
And each of them will give his life twice over
Ere one of yours shall perish. Ha! who comes?

      (*Enter* HACO, *who, seeing the crowd, hangs back.*)

Har. Haco, what news?
Hac.   News for your ear alone!
Har. Nay, let all hear! Hide they, who dare not
  show!
The first to suffer should be first to know.
Hac. The Normans are here.
Har. Here! They have landed?
Hac.   They are landing now.
Har. Are they near?
Hac.   Hear them! (*A distant shout is heard.*)
Har.   Haste then to the front!
Seize yonder hill: ye see how high it stands.
Thence, as the rocks beat back the Ocean's surge,
So we the Norman. Say, this side is England;
Beyond, that stolen strip of English ground,
That parted limb, that captive exiled brother,
Yearning to join its bleeding trunk again,
Shall yet be ours; if not in life, in death

We'll win it for our graves. Haste then! And you,
You, whom we came to succour, help to save!
Go, youth, dig trenches! Age, behind them weave
Thick-woven breastworks! Women, who have strength,
Be men and help! Who cannot work, say prayers!
All shall bear part. By heaven, my bosom burns
That Norman foot should tread on English ground
But for one hour, and we, as men in dreams,
Should natheless sleep, and nightbound suffer still
Our honour unavenged. No more of words!
I hold you back, who are on fire to go:
Quick, and reconquer England from the foe!

> (*Exeunt soldiers and villagers, shouting:* 'A Harold!
> A Harold!')

Har. Is there no place where we can talk awhile?
Gurth, Haco, stay!

G. There is a cottage here,
And this good man will give us shelter.

Farmer. Aye,
And welcome, Sirs! Come this way! Welcome, Sirs!

> (*Exeunt, while soldiers are departing, and soon again
> re-enter, with farmer, who puts chairs, &c. And
> then says,*

Scene IV.

(*Interior of Cottage.*)

Farmer. And is there anything I can do for your
Majesty? My best, Sirs, and you shall have it!

Har. Nothing, thank you, my good friend, we must be
alone.

Farmer. Aye, of course! of course! His good friend! The people's King! Good e'en to you, gentlemen! Good e'en!   (*Exit.*

Har. Now for the worst! Speak, Haco! They are come?

Hac. With the whole might and power of Normandy.

Har. Where was our fleet?

Hac.   A phantom chasing phantoms;
Or, battered hulls, in harbour tempest-bound.

Har. Their order was as bulldogs of the deep
To grip them fast. They should have perished rather,
Sunk in the wild and stormy elements,
Than quit their hold.

G.   The very winds fight for him.

Hac. Fair and foul weather, Norman, Dane, at once!
Who singly can contend such mighty odds?

Har. Our Alfred won with greater odds than these.

Hac. You jest.

Har.   Not, if our aids expected come.

Hac. Our aids? From heaven?

Har.   More near, from Mercia, Ha!
Hast thou forgot my kinsmen, good at need,
Edwin and Morcar? But whom have we here?

(*Enter Messenger, with letters.* 'From the noble thanes Edwin and Morcar, Sire!')

Har. See! (*handing it*).

Hac.   Shall I read?

Har.   Read on!

Hac. 'They are grieved: it pains them to be absent at such a time: but the harvest is late: their men have not

gathered in the corn : they will be here anon.' The
traitors !

Har. Anon ! And will time, like a courtier's tongue.
Bide at their bidding ? Time 's a flying steed,
That lets the ready rider vault on his back,
The lingerer 's left lamenting. Oh ! these men,
When one arm lacking, like a palsied limb,
May wither up our whole great enterprise,
Now, to send words ! My worthy kinsmen ! Mark,
Haco, my kinsmen !

Hac.　　　　　Build on woman's faith,
Build on a quicksand !

Har.　　　　　　Should 1 die to-morrow,
See, if there be not somewhere on my heart
Deep written, Mercia ! But why stand'st thou there,
White as Lot's wife, ill-omened messenger ?

Mess. From the Bishop of Winchester, Sire !

Har. ' He would have me solemnly absolved by Holy
　　Church.'
Another, and another, and another !
Excuses hang like fevers in the air,
And cowards catch them. What ? And yet another ?

(Enter another Messenger.)

Mess. 2. From the Archbishop of York, Sire.

Har. Ha ! (*growing black as thunder.*) What ? Aylmer
closeted with the Queen ? Aylmer ? A messenger sent
off in consequence to her brothers ? Treachery !
Haco, thou'st helped me to a wife indeed.

Hac. What news ?

Har.　　　　　She undermines me on my throne ;
Runs cross and counter to my every aim ;

Plots 'gainst my life, leagues with my enemies;
Using her knowledge with a dangerous skill
To strike me in a part most vulnerable.
Was it for this I threw away a heart
Richer than pearls?

Hac.   What? Is it possible?

G. The Queen?

Har.   Who does not know her, England's Queen,
My wife, the mother of her people, she
The eye at home, as I the hand abroad,
Watching and fighting England's enemies?
Yet she, this Queen, now when invasion armed
Stands on our shores, demanding all men's service,
Sudden, at once, or else too late for ever,
Leagued with her kin, a very Dalilah,
Steals all my strength away.

Hac.   Have you the proof?

Har. See, read!

Hac.   With Aylmer? Treachery!

Har.   Had it been
My only suffering, I had borne it; nay,
Like the bold merchant hid my loss, and smiled,
Sailing fresh argosies: but the good of all,
This common bark which barely now withstands
The gathering blast, tossed like a trembling leaf
On the wild airs—now on the foamy crest,
Now in the trough—add but a featherweight,
It sinks to rise no more.

Hac.   Perfidious woman!

G. I would have given my life to aid thy cause,
And-I have given thee—

Har.   Stay! no word of her,

She had a sceptre from me, but no love;
I could not give it. Give me the letter! There!
'Tis gone. (*Tears it.*) O friends, come nearer! Let me
    feel
Some truth about me! How this solid earth
Reels, when we trust not! World, thou art too hard,
Crooked ways beat plain. O life, strange mystery!
We are the sport of chance; one moment makes,
Another mars us: and our glory's stream,
That seemed fair-bound to the everlasting floods,
A golden splendour broadening to the sun,
Ends in mere ooze: then what we should have been,
Our name, imperishable writ in brass,
Our place, our record in life's history,
Our landmark on the level flats of time,
Broken halfway, like some tall poplar, stands
A headless trunk, storm-blasted. Come!
    G.   Forgive me!
    Har. Nay, 'tis I need forgiveness. What? Give in,
Ere a blow struck? Reach me your hands! We 'll
    win
A battle yet. Brothers in love and arms,
Whose swords, ne'er drawn save in a righteous cause,
Were never sheathed till crowned with victory,
There on yon height we may defy the world.
Then, if we live to-morrow, swear henceforth
Never to scheme again.
    Hac.   There is one way—
    Har. Arch-schemer, swear!
    Hac.   With reason for our guide—
    Har. There is no guide but truth and honesty.
    G. But hear him, Harold.

Har.   He has trod so long
The zigzag path, he cannot breast upright
The straight ascent.

Hac.   Yet zigzag and straight path
Meet in one summit.

Har.   Speak! I am stretched out
As on a rack. Moments to me are years.

Hac. List then! Inert to-day, to-morrow wise,
Our custom always, England barely wakened
Stretches her giant limbs, and dreaming listens
The cry to arms. None ever found us ready;
None ever met us with our armour on;
The best half absent, that which meets the fray
Scapes by a miracle, and a triumph snatches
Ill-merited, unearned. Not so our foe.
He of more slight, but nimbler elements,
Dreaming of war, springs as he slept full-armed;
No drowsy-eyed, half-wakened interval;
And every man is at his place at once,
For hazardous swift onset.

Har.   You would counsel?—

Hac. Retreat, delay! Delay's the sluggard's friend.
Slow fires need time. Force the reluctant Norman,
As o'er a desert which the locust leaves,
In our waste track to follow! Then—

Har.   Half England
Stripped to a desert, to concentre round me
The strength, the riches of the other half!
Is that your counsel?

Hac.   Aye! Upon one cast
Will you risk all, crown, life, land, England, all?
A gambler's throw?

Har.　　　　　　　　Had I inherited
Of ancient right some old ancestral crown,
In filial affection of men's souls
So rooted firm, that, like to Holy Writ,
It dearer grew, the more men questioned it;
Or were I general to such a king,
I would retreat; but, being that I am,
A soldier, with no title but my sword,
I am not free to suffer those attaints
Which older power would scoff at.
Hac.　　　　　　　　Is this word
Thy last? To fight?
Har.　　　　　　My last! But yesterday
I might have done it; but now, together locked,
Like wrestlers in a crowning last embrace,
With sinewy grip urging each other on
To death, all passions sleeping but revenge,
One must go down, or other.
Hac.　　　　　　Yet even now
Think, where our forts, our shelters, safe retirements,
Strongholds, where beaten valour may retrieve
Lost fields, and dare new issues.
Har.　　　　　　Haco, here!
Here in our breasts with triple armour clad
Of fiery resolution. O my friends,
Once in our lives we know what men we are;
In common hours we live as common men,
Our valour not true valour; and we deem
Our father's stature greater than our own,
We cannot wear their armour. Oh! but dare,
More strongly dare! Daring it is makes men;
Daring creates us heroes, demigods:

For, as one venomed drop of apprehension .
Is paralyzing as a serpent's tongue,
So daring, like a draught of generous wine,
Is joy, is inspiration.

Hac.   It remains
Then here on Hastings field to make our stand.

Har. To the last man, the last drop in our veins,
Many or few, hopeful or desperate,
At once, to-morrow. And God defend the right!

G. Shame on the cowards absent! They must have
The sword's dread wakening, ere they quit their sleep.

Hac. Death-bed repentance, all too late to save!

G. Ruin alone will rouse them.

Har.   Gurth, enough!
Brave men think of what is, not what might be.

Hac. Grand words! But 'tis not war.

Har.   War, or no war,
Let us live grandly first, then, when we die,
Our death will be grand also.

Hac.   You are gay.

Har. I know the worst.

Hac.   Ruin and death.

Har.   The death
That heroes love; and once to know it, Haco,
Is to know something loftier in ourselves
That dares defy it, like the Spartan host
Combing their long locks at Thermopylae,
With deathsongs welcoming slaughter.

(*Enter* OFFICERS.)

Off.   Is he here?
Sire, we must have more hands.

Har. Say hearts, not hands!
Hands follow hearts. Quick then to every thorpe,
Whatever man thou see or meet withal,
Say, Harold needs him. He will come with thee.
How are our men?
Off. All hot, and full of mettle,
Panting for fight.
Har. Yet keep their fire in bounds!
Pent fires burn longest: scattered flame soon fades.
How go the breastworks?
Off. Strong, and will be stronger.
Har. Strong only? They must be impregnable;
Branch into branch inwoven, all to earth,
Till giants foiled confess their impotence.
Off. We will do all—
Har. Ye must do more than all,
More perfect make perfection. To succeed
Is to find that on which succeeding hangs,
And not to rest till it be perfected.
Now hence, some hours of busy night to borrow!
Night must be day, sleep wait until to-morrow.

(*Exit, with Officers.*)

Hac. O most pernicious, vile, accursèd woman!
G. Waste not in cursing breath we need to-morrow!
Hac. Folly beats wisdom, as the doubling hare
Outdoes the eagle. She has ruined all.
G. Say, we, our ruin!
Hac. 'Twas her work; our plan
Was wise enough.
G. Too wise! Take notice, Haco,
There is more wisdom in simplicity

Than in the cunningest contriving art
Of fine-wove statecraft. What ? To sell a brother,
Sell him for Mercia ! Were 't to do again,
Never for all the Mercias in the world,
Northumberland to boot.

Hac.   We are Fate's toys,
Her playthings first, and then her castaways :
And yet I would I had them by the throat,
Those thanes of Mercia and Northumberland.

  G. Their doom is in the future, now is ours.

  Hac. Doom ? If 'tis doomsday, then that ends up all.

  G. I grieve our act.

Hac.   Folly, to call it ours,
Who were but voices ! O accursèd woman !
Men should not marry who would govern men.

  G. Nor mar the marriage that they cannot mend ;
We forced him to it.

Hac.   We were forced withal.
There sits an envious spirit in these clouds,
Dashes our hopes, defeats our victories ;
Yet I defy her, Fortune, fury, fiend ;
Come doom, or devil, I defy them all.

  G. To rail is nought.

Hac.   Yet railing is a vent,
Lets out an ocean of unruly thoughts
That else would choke us.

  G.   Hush ! 'tis Harold comes.

(*Enter* HAROLD, *gaily.*)

  Har. Now, ye conspirators who shape my life,
Who will go with me ?

  G.   Whither ?

Har. To the front.
I cannot sleep till I have seen the foe.
G. I will go with thee.
Hac. I, to watch the work,
And spur the workers.
Har. They will need the curb,
More like, to-morrow. Go then, worthy friend,
And if thou hear some smooth-lipped subaltern
Instruct his bearded ancient how to stand,
To thrust, to foin, to hold his weapon thus,
Scouting the antique fashion, for my sake
Forget, forgive him ! (*Exit Harold with Gurth.*)
Hac. Forgive? He can forgive :
Forgetting comes not till we cease to live. (*Rushes out.*)

SCENE V.

(*Norman Camp. The Duke in front. Knights and soldiers in the background looking after their armour, Armourers hammering, &c. Enter procession of Monks chanting, with* ODO *at their head and* LANFRANC *waving banner : Acolytes in attendance. Soldiers quit their work, and move toward the front.*)

Acolytes. On your knees, when the Holy Rood
comes by.
Voices :

> Wherever he wander, wherever he roam,
> The Church of the Northman stands near to his home.
> Sancte, sancte, sancte Callixte,
> Pugna ! pugna ! pugna pro nobis !

> Our Fathers were Vikings, they ruled o'er the wave,
> Their spirits still with us, they fight from the grave ;
> Sancte, &c. ·

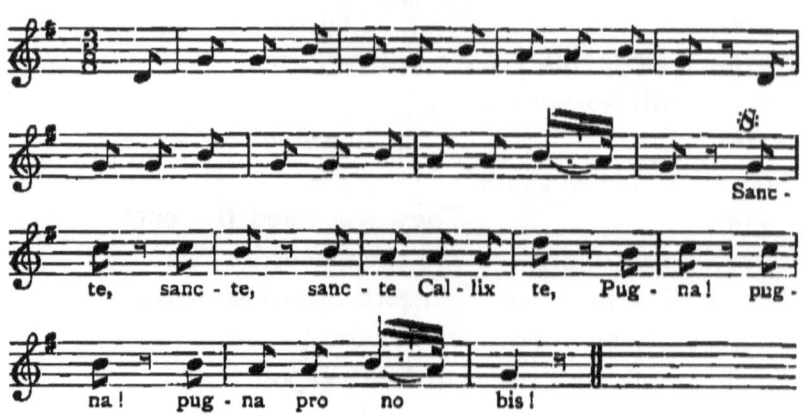

te,   sanc - te,   sanc - te Cal - lix   te,   Pug - na!   pug -

na !   pug - na   pro   no   bis !

(HAROLD, GURTH, *and* HACO *enter, and observe unseen.*)

Harold. See, see !

Gurth. What ?

Har. The Duke! Round his neck! There!

G. Harold !

Har. The oath !

G. Brother !

Har. I will confront him.

G. Stay !

Har. Unhand me !

G. Your life, your safety !

Har. My vengeance !

G. England !

Har. Ah !

Then onward, brave Normans, to battle, nor fear !
Where the onset is direst the Saints' swords are near.
        Saucte, &c. .

They pierce like the lightning, they flash thro' the gloom:
On the perjured usurper they fall like God's doom.
        Sancte, &c.

Then onward, Heaven's soldiers, to conquer or die!
If ye win, here homes wait you; if ye fall, in the sky.
　　Sancte, &c.

(Procession stops: all fall upon their knees, at a signal: the Host elevated.)

Odo. Auctoritate mea et ecclesiae peccatis omnibus vos absolvo.

G. Is this religion? Do I dream? *(turns and sees Harold still gazing on William fascinated.)* Come away, brother! This is sorcery, enchantment. This man has fascinated, bewitched you. Come!

(Curtain falls. Music still heard; the last verse repeated.)

Scene VI.

(Heath near Hastings: enter Monk, Edith *in nun's dress, and* Guide.)

Guide. I go no farther: I've lost my way.

Monk. Lost thy way! May the foul fiend take thee! But see, hast thou no landmarks? What is that dark thing beside thee, there?

G. Ah! *(rapidly moving)* Holy Mary, preserve me! What if it be he you spoke of? You'll not leave me?

M. Where is thy courage? Hark! What is that noise? A murmur as of waves! Is the sea near?

G. It should be, but I'm that puzzled—mass! I don't know!

M. Nay, it is no sea. It grows louder, though the night is calm.

G. More like, hell's awake.

M. It is a mighty army; it is the hum of men; I know it of old.

H

G. An' hark ye, there, that side! There's more of 'em. Oh! Would I were safe at home with my Bess, by my chimney-corner! Mighty little difference it makes to us, who's king in London. It's all the same down here in Mudcaster.

Edith. Is it the sea?

M. Nay, cries, and clashings, and the din of arms! We are between two mighty hosts. Ah! what is that? Some beacon, some watchfire?

G. I think, if it please your worship, Master Franklin's hayricks lie that way.

M. They have fired the villages, and as I am a sinful man, we were rushing straight into the Norman's arms. Quick, sirrah, 'tis no darkness now. Go, see if thou canst find a way.

G. 'Tis no darkness, no! But hadn't we better go together, Father?

E. Go with him! I am so wearied, I will wait here.

M. Lead on! Are you afraid?

G. Nay, I fear nothing as carries flesh and eats food. But things as is all horns an' eyes—

M. Come on then!

G. Aye, them first as knows about 'em. I'll follow.

M. (*stumbling.*) Apage Satanas!

G. Give it him well! (*Aside*) He don't like it, with all his Latin. (*Aloud*) I'm coming.

M. Courage, daughter! We shall be back anon.

(*Exit with Guide.*)

E. Aye, courage! I must live to see him still. I said the heart was dead; I would love nothing, and fear nothing, any more. But it has avenged itself. It lives a constant and a burning pain. (*Sits down and sings.*)

I know it will not ease the smart;
  I know it will increase the pain ;
'Tis torture to a wounded heart ;
  Yet, oh! to see him once again.

Tho' other lips be pressed to his,
  And other arms about him twine,
And tho' another reign in bliss
  In that true heart that once was mine ;

Yet, oh! I cry it in my grief,
  I cry it blindly in my pain,
I know it will not bring relief,
  Yet, oh! to see him once again.

(*Re-enter* MONK.)

Monk. They caught us. Our guide fought bravely, but was taken prisoner. Me they let go. We are lost.

E. Hear you? it is his voice: he is unhappy.

M. It was only the wind sighing in the branches.

E. Again!

M. It is the distant sound of armourers riveting the armour.

E. Again!

M. Truly there are wild sounds about; but who or what they are who can tell? With two such armies near, many a poor soul may have its last agony unseen, unknown. Come, and let us pray for them! (*Music heard :*

  O amare, O perire!
  O ad Deum pervenire!)

E. It is Harold! He needs me! I must go to him!

M. Thou dost not, canst not hear him.

E. Not hear him? I hear nothing else.

M. Alas, alas! She is clean distraught and gone from her mind.

E. Let us go!

M. Whither?

E. I know not.

M. We shall be lost in the darkness.

E. A light from Heaven will guide us.

M. Liers in wait will assail—

E. God will protect us.

M. I am old and weary.

E. I will hold you up. Come! (*dragging him out.*)

Scene VII.

(*English camp on downs near Hastings.*   *Enter* Grumble *and* Grub.)

Grumble. What ho, boy?

Gr. Yes, Sir.

Grum. Where is the fire that I ordered of thee?

Gr. Here, Sir!

Grum. Fire! Plague o' me! 'Tis no fire, but a smoke.

Gr. The sticks were damp, Sir.

Grum. And I have a dry cudgel here, which—
Where art going, boy?

Gr. To leave you, Sir.

Grum. And I cannot catch thee for this vile rheumatism. Nay, thou hast the legs of me, but yet can'st thou not get on without me. Let us be friends! What have we to eat? (*Grub opens a bag.*) Bull-beef again? Perdition! I would as lief eat boot-leather. And my bed, my snug hole, with straw and rushes! When I was in Wales, I had a boy, Smart, a tailor's son, who knew my measure to a hair, and could fit me as a glove. What none of these? Now I have thee, devilkin, and, plague o' me, but thou shalt suffer! (*catching him*).

Gr. Nay, Sir, Sir! There were no holes. See, I will make thee a hole. Lie thou there, and I will pile bushes round thee.

Grum. Make me a hole? Why, thou wilt make a hole of me, indeed.

Gr. And no wind shall come near thy shoulder with the dolorous—

Grum. Rheumatism. Well, I pardon thee this time. Dolorous is a good word. So, let me down softly! Eugh! But there are no rushes. What? Am I a cow to lie on grass?

Gr. I will get rushes, Sir. They grow—somewhere about here. There now (*arranging some furze about him*), thou art snug indeed.

Grum. Hm! When I was in Wales, and fought the Welshman — Away, get rushes! Begone! zounds! vanish!

Gr. If ever he see me again—

Grum. Ah! I was young then. At twenty you rush to fight, at thirty walk, at forty need other legs to carry you. Eugh! If that smoke be not in the eyes like bee-stings! But, Hillo! (*looking over the bushes.*)

(*Voices heard: enter* FARMER, GIRLS, *and* BOYS.)

Farmer. This a-way, lasses, this a-way! As sure as I'm a ruined man, they shall sup well this evening, if they never sup again.

Grum. (*aside*). Most worthy man.

Farmer. What soldier can fight empty?

Grum. (*aside*). Excellent!

Farmer. A full belly will ever beat a fasting, except in a rush.

Grum. (*aside.*) Solomon could not say it better.

Farmer. See to it then ; you, Bess, and you, Joan ! Out with the last loaf and last morsel of meat ! And, Margery, thou hast discretion, be not backward with the ale. Always drink before eating. Water the ground well before you sow seed. And, mark me now, a cup of ale between the mouthfuls is a great smoother of the way of appetite. Everything grows best in a moist ground.

Grum. (*jumping up.*) I can bide it no longer. Didst thou say ale ? Margery ! divine Margery !

(*She shrieks : he seizes the ale, and drinks.*)

Farmer. Holloa, there ! Who is it ? A Norman ? Nay, no Norman ever drank ale like that. Why, it 's a soldier, and one of the king's body-guard, God bless him ! And hungry too, I 'll warrant him. Eh ?

Grum. I could eat a goat.

Farmer. Take care of him, girls ! I 'll be back anon.

(*Exit.*)

Grum. Just a mouthful o' that meat, and then, Margery, one sip of the ale again !

Marg. Why, I thought he was a ghost, or a goblin, an' he 's drunk half a gallon o' master's best Martinmas ale, if he 's drunk a thimbleful.

Grum. I could drink a pailful of it. When I was in Wales, and fought the Welshman—

Marg. That must have been a long time ago. Are you better now, Sir ?

Grum. Better? I will fight King Charlemagne, or Knight Roland, or all the best of them, that thou, Margery, art the best ale-pourer since Ganymede. Just one cup more, fair Margery ! It spoils by keeping. If there be one thing hard to bear in a wicked world, it is thirst.

(*Re-enter* FARMER.)

Farmer. Well, girls, how is he? Got him on his legs again? Look sharp now! They are coming from the trenches. Hark to them! Singing-birds lit by glow-worms! (*Approach soldiers with torches.*)

William, a soldier, (*singing*)

> With a shovel an' a spade, an' a ditch is soon made,
>   With a stake an' a withe to bind it;
> An' a sturdy band, an' a stalwart hand,
>   With a pike or an axe behind it.

Hillo, Sir Grumble! Left us to do the hard work at the trenches? Eh! How's the rheumatism? Nay, no offence, friend! I 've seen thee fight.

Grum. And shalt see me again, if thou accost me thus.

W. Against the Normans to-morrow? Willingly! By St. George, man, I 've seen thee fight like a wild cat in our Welsh wars.

Grum. Said I not so? When I was in Wales—

W. Thou didst toast cheese upon a sword-point. But what, ho! Master Franklin again, I thought they had burnt thee out like a wasp-nest.

Frank. And so they did, my gamecock, ricks and all, above ground. But they didn't find out my inner cellar. The best part of me, like a carrot, was underground. Here, lads, roll down that big barrel yonder! Here's ale, here's meat, fit for the king, God bless him! And may the devil pick the Normans' bones! Now, lasses, help 'em round!

> (*Soldiers carouse, drinking healths; then they dance:
> one girl says,* 'Nay, Sir, fighting first, and kisses,
> an 't please you, afterwards.')

W. Eh, lass, fighting first, and, if there's aught left of us, kisses and husbands afterwards!

Grum. Nay, there's to be no marrying in England now, they say.

W. No marrying! By all the saints in heaven, why not?

Grum. There's to be an Interdict.

W. Interdict! I'd interdict 'em. Are we dogs, beasts, flies of the air or dunghill? Marry come up! Harold 'ull see to that. Pass the flagon here! Drink-hæl! Now for a song! (*Sings*)

> Come drink to my bonny brown maid!
> Come drink to my bonny brown maid!
>   For vicar or priest
>   She cares not the least,
> But she'll wed me, my bonny brown maid.
>
> So here's to my bonny brown maid,
> And here's to my bonny brown maid!
>   Tho' I lie where I fall
>   Without blessing or pall,
> She'll lament me, my bonny brown maid.

And a fig, say I, for the Interdict!

Voices. And so say I, and I.

W. And I'd sooner see a good fowl stewing in that there pot than be blessed by all the saints in the calendar.

Voices. And so would I, and I.

W. And a fig, say I, for those Normans! It was a good thought to let 'em all land here; for now we've got 'em in a trap like. I never saw a Norman yet as I couldn't crush in my hand, as if he were an egg. They're a thin, undersized set of fellows, as bald as coots, and as lean as radishes; they won't stand a good stout push, when you once get near 'em. But who's this a-coming? Hillo! Jack the falconer! a little the worse for liquor! Stay, I'll play him a trick. Halt! Who goes there? (*seizing bow and arrow*).

Jack (*carrying black jack under his arm*). Eh!

W. The word!

J. The word?

W. Yes, fellow, the pass-word!

J. Blest if I remember! It wasn't cress, it wasn't holly! Hanged if I know! Shoot and be— I'm honest Jack the falconer, and I'm all for Harold and Holy Cross.

W. Well, and that is the word. Bravo, Jack! Well said, bully Jack! Don't you know me?

J. Is that you, William? Well now! How you frightened me! I thought I were fallen among them Normans, and I'd like to ha' spilt all this good liquor.

W. Good liquor? Here; let's have it: I 'll see it 's not spilt for you.

J. No, thank you, that 's my sleeping draught. It was heavy enough when I started; but either it 's got lighter, or I 've got stronger, as we came along.

W. We! Who 's the other, Jack?

Grum. Why, his black namesake under the arm there. Two Jacks, and one of 'em drunk!

J. No, William, I'm not drunk. I see you well enough. You 're one, but—how 's that? You 've two shadows.

Voices. Bravo! Bravo, the falconer!

J. No, I tell you, I 'm not drunk, and I 'll swear it before any justiss o' the peace in England. There 's one shadow, and—there 's another shadow.

W. And three, and four, and fifty shadows, by that reckoning. Well, never mind! At all events I've not two faces, or two hearts, you'll grant me that.

J. No! You're as single-hearted a fellow as one can be who's been twice married. But those shadows! I see what it is, William. You've been drinking, and you're not the same man drunk as you are sober : you look double. But, hillo! It's bedtime, lads. There's somebody yawning. And we've got to fight to-morrow (*falls down*). And who's that tumbled? It wasn't me, for I'm here. But—put that cask under my head, someone! I'll run you, or fight you, or sleep you (*falls asleep*).

W. With any man in Christendom to-morrow! But you must sleep first, Jack. Not all the pikes and lances in this mortal world will wake thee now, till the drink is out. There, take him away! Gently! And now come, are you all good men of Kent here?

Voices. All!

W. Never a false man among you?

Voices. Never a one!

W. Come then, fill up, and I'll give you a song, and you join in when the time comes! (*sings*)

When o'er the Forelands the storm-cloud is thickening,
  When the loud trumpet is pealing afar,
When to the spoil the fierce warships are quickening,
  Forward then, Men of Kent, forward to war!

When thro' the darkness the beacon-light flashing,
  Shines over Brightling-head clear as a star,
Then, as the breakers on Dungeness dashing,
  Forward, ye Men of Kent, forward to war!

Come from your hoplands, from rich mead and river,
  Stand in the front, the invader to bar!
Let cowards shrink and go backward! but never,
  Never, ye Men of Kent, fail from the war!

    (*They drink. Shouts of* Drink-hæl! Was-hæl!)

    (*Enter* HAROLD, GURTH, HACO, *attended.*)

Har. Ah, you 're merry, my gallant men, and in good stomach for the fight to-morrow.

W. Stomach, aye, Sir King! We dined off Danes at Stamford Bridge, and now we'll sup off Normans at Hastings.

Har. Good, yet no rashness! Rashness is not valour. You must keep within these fences. English soldiers, remember, behind English oak! You will be trampled down by their cavalry in the open.

W. Eh, well, I hope I will remember.

Har. Keep behind these breastworks! Meet them with pike and spear when they charge. Lop them down with sword and battle-axe, when they climb. And then, when I give the word to charge, up, and follow me. There are too many of them to play with.

W. Many or few, they 've no Harold.

    (*Shouts of* ' No! No!' 'A Harold! A Harold!')

(*Enter* DE GRAVILLE *and* HUGUES MAIGROT, *followed by English Thanes, &c.*

Har. But who comes here? De Graville? Ye are
    come.

Monk. From William, claimant of the throne of
    England,
To Harold, his sworn liegeman.

Har.   Insolent!

What says your master, Duke of Normandy,
To Harold, king of England?

   Monk.   Still admitting
That title under protest—Art thou. king?
Then what thou hast to enjoy, thou hast to render.
Give therefore up, according to thine oath,
The throne of England to its lawful master!
Thy promise binds thee, and thine oath compels thee.

   Har. The crown of England is not mine to give;
It is enfeoffed to me, a people's trust,
And were I churlish so to cast it off,
As careless diver letting drop a pearl,
'Twould straightway fall into its source again.
And for my oath—O Sirs! What devil's here,
Upbraiding fraud, pretending sanctimony,
Against whose blackness, whose infernal hue,
My whiter fault shows purity itself,
A moon in cloud to all the night behind?
Out on him, he to speak of perfidy!

   De G. Fear not! Duke William can defend his
      honour;
Yet, if thou wilt not hear when honour calls thee,
Loth were he in such quarrel blood should flow,
Save his or thine. He dares thee meet him here,
 Alone, on foot, both armies looking on,
And to that combat's all-deciding issue,
He dares entrust his fortune and his claims.
There lies his gage.

   Gurth.   Let me!   (*offering to pick it up*).

   Har.   Avenge my honour?

   G. The king's!

   Har.   The king commands thee, touch it not!

Mine was the challenge. O my dream, how oft
Through mists of hatred, bloodshot with revenge,
I saw this hour! And now—One of us two
To-morrow shall sleep calm. But what? Ye murmur,
Your eyes look strange, my friends and countrymen.

A Thane. A nation is not as a popinjay
Shot for at fair, or market.

Thane 2. Nor a prize
In tourney-lists by gallants tilted for.

Har. Ha! would ye check me?

Thane 1. Sire, it is not equal.
You stake—

Har. My life!

Thane 1. Our all!

Har. Is honour nothing;
Stained at the fountain-head, whose stain descends
On you my subjects?

Thane 2. Sire, we love your honour.

Har. Aye, as ye love your silver, which ye hoard
Regardless of its tarnish.

Thane 1. Risk your life!
It is your own to give or lose; but, Sire,
You shall not risk our England.

Har. (after a pause). 'Tis their answer,
I could have wished it different. Breast to breast,
This battle-axe my weapon, God my trust;
He had not failed me or my righteous cause.

De G. This is your answer then; you will not meet
him?

Har. Meet him! I'll meet him at an army's head,
Where most befits a general. Yet, De Graville—
Stars in their courses sometimes cross and mingle—

Seeks he yet more? Tell him on yonder mound,
Where floats my banner, there I take my stand
Rooted till death; and, dares he fight a man
Whose life he has darkened, there he'll find me still
Burning to meet him, to hurl traitor back
To his false teeth, then on his caitiff crest
Strike hard for England, and my great revenge.

    De G. Sire, you have said. The Duke shall hear
      your answer.
Now, Monk, your duty!

    Monk.   Since thou hast no fear
To break that oath by saint and martyr witnessed,
Hear now the sovereign Pontiff, he who bears
The awful keys, that shut and open heaven,
Mightier than kings! Thou art accursèd, Harold,
Thou and thy people, all. No lawful issue
Spring from your loins! Sky, earth, and air your foes,
Mildew and mouldworm gnaw and blast your plains!
What famine leaves diseases swallow after!
Cursèd in life, then, life's long trouble over,
Death shovel down your unblest carrion!
St. Peter's blessing marches with the Norman;
Go on! Ye move like Judas to your doom.
           (*Murmurs from the soldiers 'The Interdict.'*)

    Har. (*striding forward with uplifted arm*).
Darest thou, blasphemer?

    Gurth.   Harold!

    Har.   Shall he live
Who mocks me thus?

    G.   He cannot hurt thee.

    Har.   Here,
Before my soldiers!

G. (*interposing*).   Brother, nay !. And thou,
Whose papal airs and maledictions shock
The ear of heaven, go, frighten timid dupes,
Scare softer climes ! you madden Englishmen.
How, Sirs, has Rome in matters temporal
Authority in England ?

Voices.   Never ! Never !

Thane.   There never was, or shall be, in this realm
Authority to enforce us choose our king ;
Hence with the monk ! We'll hear no more of him.

G.   Hence, pallid, hueless, wandering shape of evil !
Hence, miscreant mischief, prophet of illwill !
Hence to the shades, unfit for light of day !

Har.   Thanks, Gurth ! I was not master of myself.
When ministers of mercy so forget
Their holier task, we men of flesh and blood
May stand excused for thoughts of violence.
But you, De Graville, you ! I loved you once,
And do not hate you now. Go, tell your Duke,
There is one thing in England that we prize
More than fantastic high discourse of honour,
An honest man. That he should covet England,
I blame him not : but thus his greed to cover
With saintliest gloss, and, like the pious villain,
Throw over all the mantle of religion—
Begone ! I sicken of your specious words.

De G.   Farewell, Sir King ! We soon shall meet again.

Har.   Aye, on the field of battle ! (*To an officer*)   See
    them safe !
I would not any harm befel them here
In this our camp.

                        (Exeunt De Graville and Monk, guarded.)

                    O friends, in yonder host
I saw the priest hound on the murderer,
The while the robber and the invader knelt
To draw down blessing on their impious arms.
Go you, fear nothing! Yon proud interdict
That apes heaven's thunder, and with mortal throat
Claims for its puny breath a power divine,
To higher ears than ours sounds blasphemy;
God keeps His thunder for Himself alone.

   Thane. Fear not! We know them, and their naughty
   ways.
How little do they know our English heart,
To think us dupes of such hypocrisies!

   Har. Go then, sleep soundly! and when earliest
   dawn
Springs in the East, and every ruddy limb
Is up, aflame e'en to the finger-tips,
Then whet your courage on the rising sun!
Then, all exhilarate with valiant dreams,
Spring you to arms! Come all and stand with me,
Your swords yet bloody from the vanquished Dane,
Here on this height; and, where I set you, stand
Rooted and steadfast. Steadfast is your name;
Steadfast your boast down a long line of glory.
England no other fortress has, nor needs,
Save the stout heart, the strong arm, of her sons;
Your bosoms are her bulwark. Come then all,
Swear, she shall not be poorer for this day!
For, if we live, she shall have fame enough;
And, if we die, we will enrich her so
With seeds of noblest valour, that her soil
Shall native grow to feats of hardihood:

And on the name of England never stain
Shall briefly rest, but shall grow clear again:
And they who conquer her shall conquered be
By her unconquerable constancy.
And now, no more of wassail! Go, and sleep!
Fear not! You fight for England, and her King.
    (*Exeunt soldiers with shouts,* 'God save the King!')
  Har. Haco, see all is quiet in the camp!
  Hac. (*kneeling*). Forgive me!
  Har.   I forgive thee?
  Hac.   All the ill
I did thee, thy true love's down-trampled flower,
A stinging-nettle planted in its stead,
With perilous suggestions, downward ways
Commended, not the eagle's track and thine:
And yet, believe, I swear it on this sword,
In love I did it.
  Har.   And that covers all.
Oh, Haco, 'tis the plague and curse of life,
Where we would bless to bring calamity
On those we love; and still, the more we cherish,
The more we smooth the pathway, and avoid
The natural steep, the difficult way of things,
Purblind, impersonating Providence,
The more we make the misery of their lives.
I too have known this. Go! Farewell! To-morrow!
                     (*Exit* Haco.)
Come, Gurth! (*Sits beside his tent, covering his face with his hands.*)
  Gurth. You are troubled?
  Har.   Spite of light and reason!
Time was, I went to battle as a feast,

Gay as a bridegroom, light as thistledown;
But now—
    G.   The oath still haunts you?
    Har.   Haunt? O God,
Would that were all! It is a part of me.
    G. Those dead men's bones revived the memory?
    Har. They did: I see them ever, and the eye
Closes in vain. I see them there. Avaunt!
    G. (*kneeling*). Brother!
    Har.   What is it?
    G.   That cold treacherous man
Has you in chain: you cannot shake it off.
    Har. Only with death!
    G.   You burn to meet with him
As knight: your oath restrains you, being king?
    Har. So then—
    G.   So then, let others fight for you!
Nay, Harold, we'll not shame you.
    Har.   This from you?
    G. What?
    Har.   I of all men absent from the fight!
    G. Why not? The person of a king is sacred.
    Har. Yes, if he do his duty as a king,
The first to take, the last to quit the field.
Better a monarch dead than recreant!
    G. But if all men desire, implore it of you?
    Har. To praise me now, then twit me afterwards!
Already some condemn my broken oath;
Could I endure in honest English eyes
To read unuttered taunt of cowardice?
I cannot do it. Lurked there a hundred deaths
In yon dark field, my fate impels me on.

G. Stay, Stay!

Har. I cannot. Fate is more than man.

G. O for a hundred lives to give for you!

Har. Better to keep them all to give for England!
(*Leading him forward.*)

See, brother, see yon pair of heavenly stars!
Dost thou remember how as wondering boys
We likened them to our two destinies,
So linked together in their upward rise,
So linked too in their fall. Thus will it be,
I feel it, now. To-morrow we shall mount
The sky of fame together, and there sit
In glory crowned, on that high pinnacle;
Or, fallen together, on yon fatal field
Lie stretched to rise no more. And now, good
    night!
These fears are of the darkness, not the dawn,
To-morrow with the sun's reawakened beam
I shall be calm as thou art. Brother, good night.
(*They embrace: Gurth exit. Harold walks about,
    gazing on the stars, and great comet then shining.*)
So, peace at last! And yet Creation's sigh
Sounds in my ears. There's turmoil in the air,
On earth, on sea. Night-ravens croak around
Nature in throes! Her travail's imminent.
What is to be? Did Haco give good counsel?
Do I risk England's safety but for this,
To establish Harold's honour? Answer me,
Oh, deign some answer, cold unpitying stars!
My brow is wet, though not with kindly dews:
My brain is burning, not with natural fire;
Do ye disdain my agony? They hear me;

The heavens are stirred. See yonder fiery sword [1],
Held in the grasp of some great Archangel,
Forethreatening doom ! Whose doom ? Or mine, or his ?
Speak, gentle heavens ! They speak not. And yet
      somewhere
The event is known : the Immortals unconcerned
Know that, which we trembling, and ignorant,
Hemmed in by thick impenetrable night,
Gulphs yawning round us, dark, unfathomable,
Would give our lives to wot of; but one glimpse,
One flash, albeit to blind us. Hush ! Sweet music !
Her voice ! She chides me, that with loftier faith
I ask the stars. O God, upon this people
Let not, for perjury or unfaith of mine,
Disaster come ! Mine was the sole offence :
Mine the weak heart, the trustless, timorous vow :
On me, me only, let thy judgment fall !
Save and defend my people !

(*Enter* PAGE, *with harp.*)

Come, boy, play to me that I may sleep ! (*Lies down*
      in tent, open on one side. Boy sings.)

        Come to me, dream, sweet dream !
          Come when my life is low !
        Soft as the fitful stream
          Heard when the night-winds blow !

        Come as the evening-star,
          Bright o'er the sun's decay !
        Love, from thy throne afar,
          Shine on me ! Make night day !

[1] The great comet, supposed to be Halley's comet, of that year.

Be with me in my pain !
Lift up my weight of woe !
Comfort my throbbing brain !
Come to me ! Life is low.

(Harold sleeps, and page also. Vision rises of the scene of his oath. Harold troubled. Then vision of Edith comes, and drives it away. Music heard, singing faintly,

O amare ! O perire !
O ad Deum pervenire !

He stretches out his arms, and wakes, crying 'Edith.' *She appears on the stage, murmuring* 'Harold.' *He rises, and opens his arms : she points upwards.)*

Har. Are you an angel, or—
E.   I heard you call,
And came to seek you.
Har.   Edith, in this garb ?
E. My shield, my maiden armour !
Har.   Oh ! How changed !
Still beautiful as ever, but how changed !
Pardon !
E.   What pardon ?
Har.   All the suffering hours—
E. The sweetest, loftiest hours my life has known !
Har. Pardon, that mounting upward to the throne
I left you broken-hearted at the base.
E. And your own heart ? Oh, name not happiness !
Happy whom England looks to, nations honour !
Har. Yet happier he, forsaken by all else,
Whom one heart loves !
E.   Forsaken ? This great host ?
Har. Is but a handful to our enemies.

E.   Where are the men?
Har.   At home, in idleness!
Counting their money, fattening up their beeves!
    E.   But they will come. Patience, and trust to time!
    Har.   Time, Edith, time!   We are time's veriest fools.
Time crowns the conqueror, and the hero; then
The robber, and the intriguer.   All through time!
And oft it happens that not lacking virtue,
But lacking time, in pushes of great moment,
A week, a day, an hour, when needed most,
The ungrasped sceptre from the unpractised hand
Falls, and a knave succeeds him.
    E.   Say you so?
    Har.   And all my dream, the England that should be,
The peaceful, happy England with safe shores,
Her ancient scars forgot like childish wounds,
Her future, like a river untainted yet,
From reach to reach of glory broadening down
On to immeasurable destinies,
Gone like a birth that prematurely breathes;
One sigh, then all is over.
    E.   Can it be?
Did you not teach me justice never dies;
That virtue still immortal, like the Gods,
Suffers, not perishes?   'Tis but to purge
The indolence and torpor from the blood,
The insolence and bluster from the brain,
We endure scourging.
    Har.   Aye! But on whose back
Falls the red scourge? Not on the sluggish drone,
Not on the meretricious, boastful tongue,
Not on the authors of our miseries!

'Tis we, we finer spirits who give our blood,
All, that the base may prosper.

    E.   Let them be!
We do not make them better thinking of them;
Ourselves we shall make worse. All may go well.

    Har. Well! Hast not heard?

    E.   Of what?

    Har.   Of Mercia gone.

    E. Mercia? Her Mercia!

    Har.   At our utmost need
Edwin and Morcar fail me.

    E.   Traitors twain!
I knew it, said it, saw it in my soul:
Love is avenged—

    Har.   On us who cast out love.

    E. Through us on England.

    Har.   Peace! We shall go mad
If we look backward. Edith, I have sworn,
Sworn by God's honour and His dreadful throne,
Never to let that inward snake uncoil,
Whose sting is thought, of past felicities;
Nor tread less firmly for an idiot fear
Of evils yet unborn. And yet 'twill come,
(O righteous heaven, O retribution due!
Call that not fate, which was infatuate!)
'Twill come, like Furies with their snaky hair
Unbound, lost honour, love's catastrophe,
With what I know not dire of shock and shame,
On all, on England. Hither, oh, reach thy hand,
There's magic in a touch, that's human still,
O comfortable, fond, familiar hand
To exorcise unholy thoughts away,

When fiends assail us. Girl, as I stand here,
Here wrestling with my agony all night long,
Till the great dewdrops thick make moist my brow,
There's but a hair 'twixt me and that extreme
I dread to think on.

  E.   Peace, thou man beloved!
Play to him softly, boy! He loves sweet music.

             (Boy plays.)

  Har. Betrayed, betrayed!

  E.   Yet what a host remains,
Nursing their strength as misers all night long
To spend to-morrow like to prodigals,
All in thy cause. For who so gashed and marred,
Crushed out of shape and likeness of a man,
But, let the Norman sword cut deep enough,
'Twill only find thine image rooted there;
With thy last name surviving agony.

  Har. Oh, thou couldst root an earthquake to its bed,
Or chain a whirlwind, or with magic hand
Light altar-candles from volcano's fire.

  E. Then now as once in other brighter garb
I would prevent the dewy morning-star
To pin a rose or kerchief on thy bosom,
And see thee start; so now in robe of sorrow,
(Which, being like my fortunes, yet I love,
And would not change for all the hues of summer)
I bid thee forth. Go, and in dullest hearts
Strike fire, make heroes! England all thy thought;
England thy mother, and thy mistress: lo!
Image her faint and bleeding, at her throat
The bloodstained sword; those breasts that nursed thee
  bare;

The hands that were thy playmates piteous raised,
Pleading mute-eloquent; while the savage foe,
Tiptoe to strike, yet pauses with desire,
Hideous 'twixt lust and murder.

Har. Say no more!
Thy breath inspires me, bears me strongly up
On wing of eagles. Come or life, or death,
I reck not; life is glory, death release.
But, Edith, you?

E. I'll to a nunnery,
The fight being over.

Har. 'Tis a living death.
You shall not.

E. Harold!

Har. You, in your sweet youth,
A nunnery, never!

E. It is all that's left:
The dead heart hidden in the living tomb:
Why should I cloud earth's sunlight with my woe?

Har. Is't come to this?

E. The cloister, or the home;
Life's second Eden, or life's sepulchre;
There's no third place for women.

Har. Hast thou thought
What 'tis to grow old in the instant; pass
From life and love; unseen the face of men;
No voice, no correspondence of sweet sound
Cheering thy prison-house; to be good as dead,
Buried, without the heartsease on the grave:
Have you thought of this?

E. Aye, of this, and more
I may not tell thee, of a fire within,

That must for others burn, or burn itself,
An altar-flame, or else a funeral-pyre,
Leaving behind dead ashes.

Har.   ·Oh, lost, lost!
Rome, thou hast conquered yet a second time.
But stay, one word! If I should die to-morrow,
Live not to grow, as those who live too long,
Aged, thy beauty cankered with decay!
I should not know thee in the courts above
Less sweet, less perfect. Let us die together,
Die, and embosomed on some passionless cloud
Float into bliss! There is no bliss alone,
Alone, all memory, all regret, all tears.
Promise!

E.   If thou must die, we die together.
Farewell!

Har.   A little longer!

E. \   Night's faint stars
Burn low, and the chill breath of wakening morn,
Like the cold doomsman's summons, rude and near,
Bids me begone.

Har.   Out in the darkness? Nay,
Stay with me, let me shield thee! There, out there,
Who will protect thee?

E.   He in Whom I trust!
Look up!

Har.   Yet stay! Thy presence strengthens me;
Girl, if there were a thousand like to thee,
Ill would it fare this day with Normandy.
Ah, thou still goest.

E.   In the battle's din
My spirit shall go with thee.

Har. (*kneeling*).　　　　Then, sweet spirit,
If thou be spirit, bless me ere thou go!
　E. (*lifting up her hands*). Friend, brother, all, and more
　　than all to me!
Har.　One kiss!
E.　　　　　　Those lips are hers.
Har.　　　　　　　　And thine?
E.　　　　　　　　　　Are heaven's.
Har.　Then stooping down, sweet angel, from above,
Bring thine own heaven to calm this aching brow!
That is not her's.
　E.　　　　.　My knight! My noble one!
　　　　　　　　　　　　(*Kisses his forehead.*)
There while life lasts, still England lives in thee.
　Har.　There while thought lives, I live to think on thee.
　　　　(*Trumpets are heard: the Monk draws near.*)
Monk.　We must begone.　The enemy wakes betimes.
Har. (*fiercely*).　While England sleeps.
E.　　　　　　　She sleeps because she trusts.
I leave thee watching o'er the sleep of England.
Farewell, for ever!　　　　　　(*Exit with Monk.*)
　Har.　　　　　Till we part no more!
She trusts me; aye! and I'll deserve her trust;
Farewell, sweet friend! Come hither, sentinel!
Thou who hast watched for me this sleepless night,
　　　　　(*Sentinel approaches, and is dismissed.*)
Take now thy rest! I'll watch an hour for thee.
Now, all ye pallid fears and whileome ghosts,
Back to your dens! Come, valour-breathing morn,
With trumpet and heart-stirring clarion come,
Chasing ill dreams! Stay, wanderers of the dark!
What do ye here, when good men sleep around:

(*Gurth and Haco seen going their rounds.*)

Gurth and young Haco?

Hac.   Say, what left thee there?
Was it of earth?

Har.   Far less of earth than heaven,
Like yon blest morning. See, how bright the dawn,
Breathless, and lovely as an infant's sleep,
Laid on its mother's breast of alabaster,
Rosy and calm. How hushed, how beautiful,
Yet ushering in the wildest bloodiest day
Rose ever, big with England's destiny.
What shall it bring? I reck not. Come what will,
Or ruin, blacker than a prophet's dream;
Or triumph, mad triumphant jubilee;
Downfall, or conquest glory-garlanded;
We'll play our part; we'll brave it out as men
Set in the front, all England watching us:
And if we fail, then they who shall come after,
In far-off years fondly remembering us,
Betrayed yet true, brave but unfortunate,—
Embracing death, and in her timeless womb
Begetting countless heirs of sacrifice,—
Shall feel no shame for those who fell at Hastings,
No blush for England's soldiers and her king.
Now for the fight, a crown to lose or save,
The throne of Cerdic, or a soldier's grave!

ACT IV.

Scene I.

(On the field of Hastings, a ruined village, with villagers.)

Old man. Here I have lived for more than fifty year, to end a beggar. And the house I built with my own hands, where I brought thee, wife Margery, in the grey wimple, and red hood, on our wedding-day. Do you remember, Margery?

Margery. Aye, that I do.

Old man. And now it's all a black, black ruin, there! And my son! They have killed my son.

Marg. All gone! Nothing left for it, but to starve! And winter coming!

Old man. Those others! Why didn't they come? Why wouldn't they fight? Those others!

Child. (running to a cage, left in the ruins.) My bird! my bird! Mother, they have left my bird. Ah!
(Looking at her hands with a cry.)

Mother. What is it?

Child. Blood!

Mother. Her father's! And I got this defending him!
(Pointing to her wounded arm.)

Old man. And so young Stephen's gone. Well, he was a— *(shaking his head.)*

Marg. Aye, that he were.

Old man. Come, wife, let us be jogging!

Marg. Nay, I'll die where I lived, where my babes were born, here.

Old man. Well, there's one comfort. We're all of a piece. One's as bad off as another. What say you, Gaffer?

Old man 2. Why do they leave the old to bury the young? Why not kill all together? But who's yon? A priest, and nun! Just in time to pray for 'em!

(*Enter* EDITH *and* MONK.)

Monk. We can go no farther, daughter. Here shall you kneel, and pray for Harold.

E. But where? How can I see him? Hark! It is the fight, hard by.

M. There, on that mound! You will see all there.

E. And you? You have been a soldier, father; have worn helmet, and carried sword.

M. In my old carnal days, my days of sin.

E. And now?

M. The charred log dreads the fire. Tempt me no farther! Mount then you only! From that vantage-ground you will see all.

(*Edith mounts, while Monk sits, and tells his beads : villagers gather round.*)

M. One, two, three, four! I hear the Abbey toll!
One, two, three, four! It tolls for evensong :
And Father Ambrose leads the holy chant,
Of peace on earth, goodwill to mortal men,
The song heaven loves. Rise up, sweet litanies!
Rise up, and at the everlasting doors,
Whose double gate lets mercy issue forth,
With war's harsh discord softly enter in!

(*Faint sound of bells, and voices.*)

E. Hist, Father, hist!

M.   Who calls me?

E.   Father, here!

M. Oh, to sing Miserere once again, .
Snug in my stall!

E.   They come; they move this way.

M. Who come?

E.   I know not. Quick! Beside me! Here!

M. I dare not.

E.   Nay, I need you. Prythee, come!

M. To pray for peace!

E.   When we have conquered war.

M. (*slowly mounting.*) Quis requiescet in monte sacro?

E. Hark! 'Tis his voice, like thunder drowning all.

Harold (*heard in the distance*)

Stand but fast, and we shall win the day yet, my merry
    men! Nothing is behind you. Stand firm!

(*Shouts of* 'Harold, and Holy Cross!' *answered by,*
    'Ho Rou, Ho Rou!' *Villagers shout,* 'Harold and
    Holy Cross!' *and last of all the Monk also.*)

M. Ha! 'Tis the battle. Young again, by heaven!

E. Do you still feel it, Father?

M.   Feel it, girl?
In every pore like sunshine! Lo, the blood
Burns in the veins: obstruction vanishes.
Oh! for the strength with which I smote the Dane.
See! The dust clears.

E.   And breaking through the mist,
Shield locked with shield in long unbroken line,
Stand England's champions.

M.   Ah! But guard it well,

That tree-topped mound, our ark, our Ararat!
That is the key, the centre.
   Villager.   Do they yield?
   M. Yield! Do yon cliffs yield when the breakers
     roar?
Horseman and rider sink beneath their blows,
Lopped head and helm, shorn like to poppy-heads,
Crimsoning the greensward. While above them still
Waves proudly England's banner.
   E.   It I wove
For Harold!
   M.   And among them, like a tower,
Stands one most like a hero.
   E.   It is he,
Harold! (*Villagers shout,* 'A Harold! A Harold!') But
     look! That cloud! And there, another!
Light flashing through them, like a sun in storm!
   M. Clouds? They are Normans: and those flashing
     lights
Helmets, not sunbeams. Sancta Maria, now
'Twere worth long years of fire in purgatory
To strike one blow, one goodly blow, for England,
Young and in arms. By heaven, they'll conquer yet.
Splendidly fought! well led! Stand only firm,
Quit not your fences, gallant Englishmen!
Ah, my old eyes! They fail me. Look you, daughter!
   E. The dust of trampling chargers swallows all.
   M. Yet look! 'Twill clear.
   E.   With lances all abreast,
They come, men, horses, banners, waving plumes,
Flushed all with sunset; see, the lightning-spears,
The level lightning, the death-darting spears;

Behind them rolls the thunder. O great God,
Pent in one mass, man's greatest and his worst
Launched at our innocent heads! I'll look no longer.
Eyes, veil your light! Knees, to your better task!
You too, good people, kneel and pray for him
Who loved you, Harold! and England! Pray for them!
  (*They kneel below: the monk holds up the Cross above:*
      they cry 'Save us! Save us!' *Sounds of the battle*
      heard in the distance: then,)
  E. Hark! It grows slacker. Now it rolls this way.
We are saved! we conquer!
  (*Flying Normans seen in the near foreground: shouts of*
      'All is lost!' 'The Duke is down: I saw it: he is
      dead!')
  Duke (*rushing in, helmet in hand.*)
Dead! Nay, he lives to make a ghost of him
Who dares fly further. What? Buy one hour's life
With shame for ever? You, old Rollo's seed,
Degenerate! You, of those tremendous sires
Bastards, not heirs! How say you, 'All is lost'?
Fools, not to know I never won a fight
But first I lost it, and my proudest triumphs,
Like hard-earned feast of starving mariners,
Were seasoned with sweet relish of despair:
So desperate seemed my fortune, till she turned
And granted all her favours. Ah, and see!
She grants them now. By heaven, they break, they
      come,
They quit their stronghold. Oh, I shall call you girls,
Not men but girls, if e'er those madmen gain
Their fences more. And now, my countrymen,
Remettled to your task with courage new,

K

Where honour calls, bright honour, with old fame,
Reaped on a hundred fields in Normandy,
Give me this day! But this one effort more!
'Tis the last arrow brings the eagle down;
'Tis the last billow wafts you to the shore;
Swear not to fail! No protestations now!
Deeds, I want deeds. From yonder armed height
Bring me a crown! Then shall ye reap reward
Richer than Alexander grasped in dreams,
Or Caesar sighed for: but this one last day:
Life is not given except for noble deeds:
Then rest for ever! then fortune, all, is yours,
And England mine. On, on to victory!

(Rushes out, followed by soldiers.)

Monk. The fearful man!

E.   What born of flesh and blood
Can stand against him?

M.   Look! I cannot see.
Come they still onward?

E.   Now they see their fault.
They waver, pause: their leaders force them back.

Villager. Whom?

E. Our brave soldiers! They as stubborn mastiffs,
Shoulder to shoulder, fronting still the foe,
As though for each foot backward they would go
Still forward ten, yield slowly! Quicker! Oh,
Quicker, brave hearts! They are near you. At your
    heels
The weltering flood! It is a race for life:
Who wins, wins England. Laggards! Now, at last
Your shelter reached, in with you! Ah, too late!
Too late! The knights are on them. Trampled down,

Hoof-trodden, crushed, torn, mangled! Beast to man,
Not breast to breast, Norman to Englishman!
This is not battle! Few regain the mound;
Few, but all heroes. Hark!

Har.   Stand firm, and fear not!
Still am I with you.

Duke.   Fools! Shoot higher, higher!
Not in the wood, but up to heaven, to fall
Like doom upon them! In their faces! Thus!
Kill, kill! Night comes. Now or never!

                           (A great cry heard.)

E.   Ah! 'Tis over.
That was his voice: his mighty heart there broke.
And all is ended, and the sun goes down.
O Harold, England!

    *(Covers her face with her hands: Norman women, with
        knives and torches, rush on the stage, shrieking 'To
        the slaughter!')*

M. Spirits of night, their hellish work begins.

                    (Curtain falls. Sad music heard.)

Scene II.

(Room at Chichester, not far from the battle, belonging to Simon,
a Jew.)

Simon. They are at it, now, hard by, on the field of
Hastings. Norman hammer on Saxon anvil: Saxon
pole-axe on Norman head-piece. Which will hammer
longest, and hardest? And which, when it is over, will
come to old Simon, to lend him moneys? Ah, I like not
this fighting, these wars. 'Tis ill fishing in troubled

waters. A wrong cast to this side, or that side, and you
may lose all. See now, (*takes out one of Harold's coins*)
'Harold, Pax.' That is good. Would it were peace
everywhere! Then are the rents paid, and the moneys
come in, and the poor Jew gets his own. Holy Moses,
what was that? (*hastily hides the coin.*) It was nothing.
A mouse! Crumbs from my yesterday's dinner! I am
undone with mice. What be the cats doing? Truly a
good peace, with moneys wanted everywhere, at good
interest, and on good security, that were not far from
Paradise! Ah! (*knock at the door*)

(*Enter two Gentlemen, muffled, one young, one older.*)

Gent. 1. Simon, we want money.

S. And where should I find moneys in times like
these?

Gent. 1. In that strong box, or the hole in the wall
yonder, or in that chimney-corner beneath the hearth-
stone : or (*shakes him*) Heavens, how he rattles! He is
made of gold.

S. Nay, gentlemen, good gentlemen, my keys! (*pro-
ducing them*) do not rob me!

Gent. 1. Not if you'll use your keys to unlock those
strong boxes. Come, Simon, don't be greedy! We don't
want to rob you, but money we must have.

S. And for what should you want moneys?

Gent. 1. Why to go fighting, to be sure! to help
Harold against the Normans.

S. You are too late. They are fighting now.

Gent. 2. What? Now, Simon? How know you that?

S. Enough, I know it. You may count upon it, as on
your Gospels. While we stand here, they are fighting

yonder (*they show amazement*). Why did you not go yesterday?

Gent. 1. Well, yesterday, to speak truth, I was drawing a badger.

S. Father Abraham, a badger! And he will fight for his hole, will he not?

Gent. 1. Of course he will, fight to the death. That is the fun of it.

S. The fun of it! A poor beast, having no more sense than a badger, will yet fight for his hole, to the death. And you, English, will not fight for your fine country, till it is too late. And you want moneys? (*After a pause*) And what shall be my security?

Gent. 2. I, old Simon. I will pledge part of my land for this young friend of mine, to buy him horse and harness; and that I think is security, even for you.

S. Security? Yes! Good enough till the Normans take it.

Gent. 1. Come you screw, you Jacob-seed, you old bloodsucker, give us the money at once, or else—(*a tap heard at the window*).

S. Stay a little! (*goes to the window, and takes in a message brought by a horseman*). A message from my Sarah, gentlemen! By your leave! (*reads hastily*)

'Harold is winning: the Normans lie thick upon the field: will send later tidings by fire-signals, as agreed.

Yours, ISAAC.'

Good! Gentlemen! And you would have moneys on good security, his land: and on good interest.

Gent. 1. By which you mean monstrous usury. No, I cannot allow that.

Gent. 2. No matter, Wilfred, it is no great matter: I

can still afford it. (*A slight altercation between them, during which Simon brings out a bag of money, with pen and parchment.*)

S. See, here are the moneys. And here is a little bond, a small matter, which you will each sign for me. There I will give you light to see it. You shall write your names down here. (*Moves a lamp towards them.*) Stay! You did say the land should be my security. Which land?

Gent. 2. The woodland! You've had most of the rest before.

S. The woodland! Good! I like that, for wood is money. (*Aside*) That signal!

Gent. 2. But quick! Your parchment!

S. That signal! (*aside*). What, you would have in one moment what took me years to gather?

Gent. 1. Out of our plunder, our very bones.

S. Aye, while I saved what you wasted.

Gent. 1. Quick!

S. Stay! (*Aside*) Will that signal never come? You would have the money now?

Gent. 1. Instantly!

S. Instantly? There must be some abatement for instantly. For a hundred pounds you shall have fifty. See now!

Gent. 1. You thief, you curmudgeon, you—

S. As you will, gentlemen! Why do you come to me—

Gent. 1. Because you have what we want.

Gent. 2. Nay, Wilfrid, we waste time. Give me the parchment! (*He is about to sign when a light flashes in at the window.*)

S. There! Stay! (*seizes on the parchment.*)

Gent. 1 and 2. What was that? Is it a house on fire? There, let us finish it!

S. Nay! It is my signal. One fire! 'The Normans are gaining ground.' (*A second light, during which persons rush in, crying,* 'What is it? What news, Simon?') Two fires! 'The English are defeated.' If it come again, it is all over with you. (*A third light: Simon leaps up with frantic haste, seizing his money*) 'Harold is dead.' Moneys, I give you moneys? Never! Out, sluggards! Ye are too late. Begone! Your Harold is no more. Ye should have helped him yesterday. And this now (*shaking his money*) is not for you, but for the Norman. And Heaven help the poor plundered, preyed on, persecuted Jew! (*drives them out*).

Scene III.

(*The field of Hastings.* WILLIAM *and his troops, torchlight.*)

Fitzosborne. We pray you, Sire, accept the crown of
    England,
Fallen from the usurper, found on yonder plain!
And as our fathers did, on battlefield,
Elect their worthiest sovereign whom to serve :
So we thy knights, thy nobles, greet our King,
Long life and hail, William the Conqueror!

    Barons. And we thy barons swear to guard the
    Crown,
Our swords, our honour, and our faith upon it!

Odo. And holy Church doth consecrate the Crown,
Her grace, her blessing, and her prayers upon it !
   Soldiers. And we thy soldiers swear to serve the
    Crown,
Our blood, our service, and our lives upon it !
   Duke (lifting the crown.) These hands are bloody that
    do grasp the Crown,
Yet bloodier, see, the Crown from him who bore it,
Bloodiest of all, the field whereon 'twas won.
So be it ! Since ye would not come in peace
Under my yoke, stiff-necked Englishmen,
Now pay the forfeit and full cost of war !
This be my prize ! All else in this fair realm,
Its shadowy forests, its well-watered meads,
Its fat flocks ranging white o'er boundless plains,
City and wall, old castles grey with time,
Wide fields, rich manors, joyous pleasances,
With streams, thro' which the flooding ocean pours
Bringing earth's wealth from far-off continents :
All this be yours ! Take it, but under pledge,
To guard it ! Force at length doth govern all :
Force, only sovereign till a stronger come :
And freedom, like a jealous mistress, claims
Obedience, order, union of the free,
Service, and over all one Head supreme,
So that who touches one man, injures all.
Then where these English, like their native oaks,
Stood single, sheltering each his separate field,
There do ye, warders of a larger good,
Who fight, not for a part, but for a whole,
A people ready, a nation all in arms,
Stand fast in ranks, each ordered, all combined,

Links of a vast embattled harmony;
Guard well your coasts, watch every wind that blows,
Suspect the very breakers round your shores,
Lest they be leagued to admit your enemies!
Cover with armèd fleets your subject seas!
Be strong, be daring, yet be provident!
And then far hence, in ages yet to come,
Saxon with Norman, Nature's sturdiest growth
With graft of happier blending, ye shall grow
Into one race, one people, whose great heirs
Filled with a fierce yet unconsuming fire,
An iron race, a race indomitable,
With souls too large for these our island-bounds,
Shall hence go forth to subjugate the world!

(*Enter two seeming Monks, one of them* EDITH *in disguise.*)

De Graville. Two poor old monks' from Waltham,
   gracious Sire,
Would see your Highness.
   Duke.   What would you?
   Monk.   Sire, a boon!
   Duke. If it may rightly stand with England's honour,
The boon is thine.
   Monk.   We ask you, Sire, for leave
To search the field, and 'mid the slain discover
The corpse of Harold.
   Duke.   What!
   Monk.   To take it hence
To Waltham, where the monks his bounty fed,
Shall evermore sing masses for his soul.
   Duke. God's splendour! no! He lies beneath the ban.
Living he did offend of sacrilege,

And where high Heaven o'ertook him, let him lie !
No grass will grow upon a perjurer's grave.

   Monk. Yet, Sire, have mercy ! If hard-judging Justice
Be thus extreme to punish each offence,
What man is he would merit burial ?

   Duke. Begone ! I will not suffer it.

   De Graville.   Nay, my liege,
Let me beseech you !

   Duke.   You ! De Graville !

   De G.   Sire !
While Harold lived, I held him recreant,
False knight and traitor to his oath : his greatness,
Like stars that make night's blackness yet more black,
Did but make greater his offence ; but now,
Now he is gone, we war not with the dead ;
In his own Abbey let him lie and sleep,
And these old men with masses shrive his soul !

   Duke. De Graville, no ! Harold indeed is dead,
But his cause lives : the viper-blood still breathes ;
Wherever foot is set, a serpent stings ;
And what if thus entombed in Waltham's pile,
A halo spread about his guilty bones,
He grow a saint, heroic, canonized,
Sacred the very stillness round his tomb,
While mourning myriads, pilgrims to his shrine,
Thence shall return, rebels and traitorous :
Until a ghostly rival pluck me down,
A spectre rise, and thrust me from my chair ?

   De G. Nay, Sire ! I ask but this, reward of all,
Payment in full of all my services.

   Duke. Too much ! In England there are soldiers still,
Twenty to one, to those we conquer'd here.

De G. Yet—

Duke.   Let all things ill-omened prey on him!
Kites of the air are fitting traitor's tomb;
Here let him lie: no man to bury him!

Edith. What, no man?

Duke.   None!

Edith. (*throwing off her hood and cloak*). Then let a
    woman plead!

Plead angels for me! Saints inspire my tongue!
Kites feed on Harold? carrion birds of air
Touch his dear head? Nay, Sire, tho' daring all,
By heaven, you dare not outrage thus the dead!

Duke. Dare not? I dare not? Let me hear a man
Say, dare not, to me!

Edith.   If he erred, it was
That he loved England; and shall he alone
In England lie unburied?

Duke.   Who is it?

De G. Alas! the Lady Edith!

E.   Rather say,
In times far hence, happy and fortunate,
I was the Lady Edith whom you knew,
Flattered of all; in camp and tournament
A theme of minstrelsy, a light of song;—
Forgive me, heaven, recalling happier days!—
Now but a dream, a ghost, I wander here,
Dream of past bliss, ghost of remembered joys,
Pale sorrow's shadow led by old despair,
Dead to all else, still living but for this,
To find out Harold, and to bury him.

Duke. Lady, my word is spoken.

E.   Yet that word

Can be recalled. See, I do make appeal
To all men here : brave knights, if valour move you,
Priests, in the name of Christian charities,
Sirs, all, if aught of human in you dwell,
Some tenderer spot, some softer memory,
Not stiffen'd and grown hard with strokes of war,
Pity the fallen ! Oh, yes, you are not stones,
You would not I should sit as Rizpah here,
Alone with tempests, and the wintry moon,
Her princes slain, her heart a sepulchre,
Scaring the foul night-ravens from their prey.

                (*Signs of emotion among those present.*)

Oh, thanks ! Those gracious and relenting tears
Give what I ask. You will restore him to me :
Be brave, yet, true to knighthood's loftier vow,
Be gentle ; chivalry loves gentleness :
And grant me in these true and tender arms
To bear him hence, and in some holy place,
Where men abide the Judgment, lay him down,
Then sit beside his tomb, and weep for him.

    Voices. 1. Let her have the body.

    2. He slew my brother, yet I would not deny him
Christian burial.

    3. We war not with women.

    Odo. Yield, brother ! It were well. Press not too far
A right undoubted ! 'Gainst the public sense
To damn his memory were to hallow it.

    Duke. Yield ? I !

    O.   Who yields not is o'erthrown at last.

    Duke. Thou too against me !

    O.   For thy good alone !
Nay, mighty lord, what turmoil o'er a tomb !

Would that the earth were larger, wide enough
To find a tomb for all our enemies!
I could have pity to embrace them all.
Thus far have mercy!

Duke.   So, the Church has spoken.
Thou hast prevailed. Go, find and bury him!
Thou too, De Graville, and Fitzosborne, go,
(A gift is nothing if not generous),
Wait on her, aid her in her search, and all,
All that she needs, provide her! And, good Sirs,
When we too die—and death is near to all;
It overtakes us in the quiet field
No less than in the battle's butchery—
May love as faithful fitly tend our bones!
Lady, they wait thy bidding.

    (*Exeunt Monk, Edith, De Graville, and Fitzosborne.*)

Duke. Now, whence we started with the morning star,
Thither return we victors, late at eve.
Back to your tents! the wounded on your shields
Bear softly! Glorious are the strokes of war.
The common man they lift to be a peer,
The peer to prince, the prince to paladin:
For everyone may win his spur of gold,
And nameless turn to noblest on the field.
While on the dead let silence softly sleep,
Here where they fell. To-morrow, with the dawn,
Ere the new trumpet, herald of fresh fame,
Bid us forget old griefs of yesterday,—
Our laurel'd triumph twined with cypress-leaves,—
We will return with pomp to bury them.
Now sound loud clarions, and triumphant tell
How William conquered, and how Harold fell.

    (*Martial music, during which exeunt omnes.*)

Scene IV.

*(*De Graville, Fitzosborne, Monk, Edith, *and soldiers, on the battlefield.)*

De G. This way! Let me assist you, Lady! (*She repels him.*)

Monk. She has a guide, a light within. Trouble her not, but follow!

De G. The moon breaks forth, we shall have light for our task.

Soldier. Here lies Roger de Tancarville, slain in the last charge by the English King. He was a good man and true.

2nd Soldier. That was a right good blow. See! The axe struck here. It crushed his skull like a filbert.

De G. Here is the mound where stood the royal banner.

Fitz. (*picking it up*). Which one still holds, clasping it to his breast in death. All honour to the brave! True heart! gallant deed!

Edith. Gurth, Gurth! (*looking at the face*) He must be near. And young Haco too! he was ever at his side, too near him. Oh! it is coming! (*Sad music.*)

De G. Bring torches hither! Quick! Yet more of you! (*They form a semicircle.*) There! there! (*Edith falls with a shriek, swooning on Harold's body.*) 'Tis he!

Fitz. (*tries to pick her up.*) Alas, poor lady! She loved him dearly.

De G. Nay, leave her! You would but wake her to fresh sorrow. Well for her if her swoon could be eternal!

Monk. She would come here. She would have it so (*wringing his hands*). Nunc dimittas, Domine, nunc dimittas !

Edith (*waking up*). What have they done to him ? Oh, Harold ! Harold ! (*lifting him up and kissing him tenderly*). Cold ! cold ! cold, my love ! Will he not speak to me, answer me, ever again ? Never ! never ! never ! Oh, Father, can you do nothing for him ? Can you not help, plead, kneel, pray for him ? He ever loved you, ever laboured for you. He—(*the monk points upward with his upraised cross*). Oh ! dead ! dead ! dead ! Never again ! Never again ! (*Music.*)

E. And ye did it, ye slew him ! Ye robbers, brigands, murderers, ye massacred the noblest life in England ! (*to the Normans*). It was you—

Monk (*turning round*). Daughter !

E. Oh, pardon, pardon ! Nay, it was kind cruelty that did it. So long lost to me in another's arms ! and now, in death, in death at last, we are united. Belovèd ! Belovèd ! See, it grows darker, darker. Hush, who called me ? He ? This, he ? Nay, he was a goodly man. He waits me there. I come, I come. O heavenlit cloud ! O wafting arms ! Found ! and for ever ! (*Falls dead upon his body.*)

> (*Monk kneeling on one side, with outstretched arms: De Graville and Fitzosborne leaning on their swords on the other : torch-bearers behind : in the middle, Edith on Harold's body. Curtain slowly falls.*)

POEMS.

POEMS.

—◆—

THE DAY OF JUBILEE, 1887.

As men look back in after-days
Where once they trod in slippery ways,
And find fresh theme for love and praise;

And here, they tell, the snow was deep,
And there we venturous dared to creep
Along crevasses dark and deep;

And there we cut the wall of ice,
Or, desperate gamblers throwing dice
For life, we clomb the precipice:

And all the way we went along,
With spirits clear and bosoms strong,
We often wandered, oft went wrong.

One step alone, the next, we knew;
Yet still an onward instinct drew
Our progress, till, with evening dew,

As birds at twilight roosting come,
We reached our fair Italian home,
The slumbering lake, the peaceful dome.

L 2

So we, who after fifty years
Look back, remembering hopes and fears,
Melt into gratitude of tears,

For all that is ! the might-have-been
Forgot, in this her triumph-scene
When England gathers round her Queen !

For peace at home, and heard afar,
Heard only, threat of distant war,
No bloodstain here our fields to mar !

For India held with stubborn mood,
When, 'gainst the furious Sepoy-flood,
Dauntless our little leaguers stood !

Or where, on bleak Crimean height,
Nigh lost, the soldier saved the fight,
And, when chiefs blundered, brought all right !

Or where, 'mid fiend-like dervish-yell,
Betrayed, deserted, Gordon fell,
And England shuddered, as at a knell,—

Too late to save, but not to mourn ;
Yet, of one hero left forlorn,
Proud to believe a hundred born !

For something lost, yet more of gain ;
For healing arts that soften pain,
That ease the nerve, and soothe the brain !

For Nature conquered, powers of strife
Made fruitful, powers with blessing rife ;
For arts of beauty sweetening life !

For knowledge spread, and useful lore
Brought to the humblest cottage-door,
For kindlier touch 'twixt rich and poor!

For wider justice clasping all,
And, broken down the parting-wall,
One law alike to great and small!

For freedom, elsewhere snatched not given,
Here working like a wholesome leaven,
Raising the heart and opening heaven!

For these, for all; the good acquired,
The goal that once our fathers fired,
Now starting-point for good desired!

Whate'er our lot, where'er our way,
On this at last her crowning-day,
Father, to Thee we kneel and pray:—

For her, long life with glorious close,
And, dying, honoured place with those
Who lived to lighten human woes;

Who set an aureole round the crown,
And loftier rise by stooping down
Than in low heavens of war-renown!

For us, that like our sires of old,
Statesman, and soldier, seaman bold,
We may her Empire strongly hold;

Whether, now reached its farthest scope,
Our downward path begin to slope,
Or upward climb with boundless hope,

With equal heart for every fate,
Not cowering crushed by fortune's weight,
Not with prosperity elate,

But storm, or sunshine, taking all
Indifferent, save at duty's call
To meet the hour, whate'er befall.

For He Whose scales the nations weigh,
The Lord of night, the Lord of day,
Breathes, and as flowers we fade away :

And yet again, with pity stirred,
Sweet as at dawn the waking bird,
'Rejoice! arise!' his voice is heard.

So seems it still our wisest trust,
To bravely bear what bear we must,
And reverent answer, God is just.

OXFORD TO LONDON.

O Friend, who labouring for the State,
With sittings early, sittings late,
 Dost gnaw thy soul with righteous anger
At party violence, party hate :

To see our Senate's old renown
'Mid faction's darkening surges drown,
 And many a name of purer splendour
Setting, and like a star go down :

To hear the howl, the hiss, the cry,
The blatant taunt, the bandied lie,
  Where, saved through laws that guarded order,
The friends of anarchy law defy:

To long—and 'scarce to deem it sin—
To see some Cromwell enter in,
  And, England's mandate stern behind him,
For freedom's honour end discord's din.

Then come and quit the heated hall,
The strife, the mock division's call,
  Come, and amid old friends at Oxford,
In peace and beauty, forget it all!

Come, and where breaks a softer ray
On walls with centuries sere and grey,
  'Mid memories old as Saxon Alfred,
Refresh your heart with the heart of May!

In meads where couch the slumberous kine
With kingcup and with cowslip fine,
  By many a College ivy-mantled,
Trellised with rose and eglantine:

Or lawns like emerald velvet laid
'Mid whispering cloisters' dim arcade;
  And walks by student-dreamer trodden,
Leafy and cool in their elm-trees' shade:

Or, sweeter still, arched boughs between,
To trace the twilight-glimmering scene,
  The ghost-like city, steeple-studded,
Slumbering grey in a mist of green:

Or listen while the throstle sings
Night's requiem, where, yet adding rings,
　　Millennial oaks bemock the aloe,
That once a century skyward springs :

Or follow, still by fancy led,
Where bells are ringing overhead;
　　Bells with their ceaseless chime in Oxford,
Voices to warn from the peaceful dead.

Or wander down an ancient street
Where mingling ages quaintly meet,
　　Pillar and pediment, dome, and gable,
Mellowed by time to a picture sweet.

Or sit where saints have sate, and feel
Their calm across our spirits steal,
　　Their singleness, their depth of purpose :
Our lives seem shallower as we kneel.

Or stand in many a noble hall,
Where England's greatest deck the wall,
　　Prelate, and statesman, prince, and poet ;
Who hath an ear, let him hear their call !

Or pace, remote from noisier throng,
Some shadowy corridor along,
　　And tread on tombs, and waken echoes,
Bidding the living be true and strong.

Or take the oar, and down the stream,
Silently floating like a dream,
　　People the wave with phantom races,
And hear the shout for the victor-team :

Thoughts of a past, a happier time,
When selfish aim seemed public crime,
   And feel once more the pulses quicken
With generous heat of a genial prime.

Then, back returning, seek once more
The Babel city, the wordy war;
   Perchance a drooping cause to hearten,
Perchance its wavering ranks restore.

For still, though doubtful seem the fray,
And long the struggle and hard the way,
   Yet lawless passion is self-destroying,
And coolness, courage, shall win the day.

1886.

OXFORD, PAST AND PRESENT.

OH! the rush of old men with the kindly anxious faces,
   Bald heads, and white heads, or turning fast to grey;
Wandering here and there in the old familiar places,
   Knowing, alas! nothing of the Oxford of to-day!

Oh, alas! the thronging of so many men, so wrong in
   Just the very questions where so right they wish
      to go!
Women here corrupted! All our studies interrupted
   By their lightness, by their brightness! Nay, dear
      friends, it is not so.

Oxford still is Oxford, as you knew it, as you loved it;
   For its great and high ideals, ever earnest strug-
      gling on;

Women check our aim? Nay! rather they will help
    to push it farther,
  And from Oxford's light illumined light their torch,
    and hand it on.

In the quiet peaceful village, where the men are rude
    with tillage,
  In the factory's din and discord, in the dull and
    dingy town,
They will spread the light of knowledge they (as you
    did) learnt at College,
  And with bright refining touches slowly tone the
    roughness down;

Yet their charm the while unaltered! Still the joy of
    life domestic,
  Truer wife, and wiser mother, through the student's
    added lore!
If, as some one says, a woman knowing little is 'ma-
    jestic,'
  Ah! what will she be in future, when she knows a
    little more?

Then may we too grow more human, through the
    warm heart of the woman,
  Read earth's riddle with her insight, see earth's
    sorrow with her eyne;
Not, as oft, in sidings shunted, or, in darkness grop-
    ing, stunted
  Gnomes of power, but useless boring in some old
    exhausted mine.

Fare ye well then, dear opponents, (we'll not call you
    foes,) and ever,
  Ever, though in mind divided, may our hearts united
    stay!
Still, believe, we too love Oxford, only use our best
    endeavour
  To keep Oxford's touch with England, with the Eng-
    land of to-day.

    April 29, 1884.

DUTY.

CALL, and I follow, power unknown;
Thy summons has a sovereign tone,
As trumpet stern in morning air
To bid to duties fresh repair,
Or bugle soft, with evening dew,
To cleanse and fortify anew.
Call, and I follow; peace or war,
I care not what thy mandates are:
In peace, 'tis somewhere bliss to find
A stay for the unstable mind;
And 'tis in power of war alone
To strike at once the master-tone;
To break the spell, to breathe the word
More trenchant than a warrior's sword;
To chase the fear, the doubt to slay,
And cut the sophistry away;
Till out of ease, and evil fire,
The witchery of low desire,
Refashioned on a loftier plan,
Springs from the grave an altered man.

Call, and I follow, power unseen;
Thou dost not ask what I have been,
How little worthy of the prize,
How all unmeet for sacrifice;
Nor ask I what thou hast in store
Of wavering balance, less or more;
What thrill of pleasure, throb of pain,
Or nearer loss, or distant gain.
For, mighty voice, we cannot see
What is the end of following thee;
The laurel-wreath, the triumph-crown,
The hero's rapture of renown;
Or, struck to death beneath the wall,
Unseen, unknown, unwept, to fall;
Contented yet in dying ear
The victors' shout aloft to hear,
And feel, they had not climbed so high
But o'er our mortal agony.

Call, and we follow! Cold and bare,
How is it that thou art so fair?
While softer beauties leave us tame,
How dost thou set our blood aflame?
And call us from the flattering crowd,
The maddening shout, the plaudit loud,
The laugh, the lights, the flowers that shine,
The revel and the untasted wine,
Alone, apart, with thee to win
A solitary joy within;
The joy, from sources past our ken,
Of sternest souls and strongest men?
O mightiest Voice, 'tis that in thee
We join a nobler company;

And with them trust thy call to find
No empty figment of the mind,
But echo, in unearthly tone,
Of lips divine in worlds unknown.
'Tis that beneath thy poor disguise
We read a wanderer of the skies,
Whose broken utterance faint and rare
Is common-tongue of angels there.
And once it happened as we went
Companioned with a sweet content,
Listening to hear thy music strange,
Our very being seemed to change ;
The veil of flesh to fall away,
The eye to see a purer day ;
While common brook, and purling springs
Would babble of eternal things ;
Another form beside us trod,
We knew thee, Duty, power of God.

JOHN BRIGHT.

LOVED at the last ! The great Tribune, the fighter,
  The name once in England chief discord, chief fear !
Now a spell breathing peace, now a link to unite her,
  From the crown to the cottage, prince, people, and
    peer !

Loved at the last ! Lo, a nation stands mourning
  Up there in the North, 'neath his cold native skies ;
No pomp at the tomb, and no hatchment adorning,
  Plain, simple, the grave where the great Quaker lies.

Ah, there let him rest ! Do our wishes still wander
  To the Statesman's last home, the great Abbey afar ?
Nay, think ! Is not something far truer and grander
  To be even in death what we were, what we are ?

Free, free as a child, from vainglory, ambition,
  Though the charm of a senate, the first on the floor,
Still true to the cause of a life, of a mission,
  To the cause of the humble, the lowly, the poor.

There leave him ! So Rotha her Wordsworth is keeping ;
  Sir Walter lies hushed by his Tweed's native song ;
And, greatest of all, mighty Shakespeare is sleeping
  Where Avon's still waters flow softly along ;

To teach us what fame is : the city's ovation ;
  A clamour, a splendour, a bubble's brief gleam !
But the triumph was won far away, the creation
  Of life's simpler moments, by mountain and stream.

And though there was something they learned, be it
    granted,
  From fine nurture's art, not from nature's rude loam,
Yet greater by far what they brought, when trans-
    planted,
  In the strength of the soil and the breath of the
    home,

Pure, racy, and healthful. And therefore returning
  When the day's work is over, the darkness is nigh,
They come back like the soldier world-famous, but
    yearning
  In the home of their childhood heart-weary to die.

It is over. That voice! shall we ever forget it?
  That music, that language, so rich and so strong?
Milton's sword! In his hand the great Puritan set it,
    And taught him to wield it 'gainst falsehood and
      wrong;

Never drawn save in cause of some weakness down-
      trampled,
  Never sheathed till at eve the great struggle was won;
So he took it, and, armed with a power unexampled,
  He smote right and left till the battle was done.

It is done. Let him rest! We seek not to discover
  The proportion exact, what to praise, what to blame;
In a day of great heat, when the burning is over,
    Some may have been hurt, have been singed, in the
      flame:

But a greatness was there. 'Twill remain a possession
  For England's far future, to ages unborn:
And how oft in the dearth, the despair, of the Session,
  Shall we seek his great presence, his anger, his scorn!

Hard-hitter, strong fighter, but stooping to faction—
  Oh never! Oft lonely the path that he trod;
But he cared not for praise, and he feared not de-
      traction,
  Brave soldier, good worker, true servant of God.

So, loved at the last! Other love is more flying,
  In youth a fierce fever, with age cooling fast;
But the love of a nation more faithful, undying,
  Not passion, not fancy, is love to the last.

And though for a while she may blame, she may
    chide them,
  Her children, dear Mother, yet when all is past,
They may count on her justice, 'tis never denied them,
  If only they loved her, she'll love them at last.

PROGRESS.

WHAT Progress in the sum of human years?
I asked of Truth, whose wan and weary eyes,
    Fixed on the strife of hosts contending,
    The strife of Good and Evil never-ending,
    Were clouded oft with tears.
Sad as the strain of saddest symphonies
The sorrow of her answer filled my ears :—
'Daily men know me more, and love me less ;
Time was, I flashed upon the young world's sight,
And drew all hearts with wonder and delight,
    In my first loveliness.
Then a great promise o'er the distance hung,
That would make all things happy, all things young ;
    Redeem the curse, relieve the pain,
    The great world's misery heal again :
So was it echoed on from tongue to tongue.'
'And then?' I asked. She answered, 'As a star
Glad seers saw and hailed me from afar :
And suddenly a glory was revealed
    To simple shepherds in the field,
    Who saw a light in heaven, and lo!
With angel-forms the dark was all aglow,

While through the spheres a sacred music rung;
    "Peace and goodwill!" O blessed word!
"To you is born a Saviour, Christ the Lord;
    More strong than blood,
    That tie of brotherhood,
He comes to dwell his brothers here among:
    Of David's stem,
    The rose of Bethlehem,
Goodwill and peace!" To all the promise sung.'
'And now?' I asked. No answer! 'Now?' She
    turned,
And all her cheek one fire of anger burned;
She felt the strong weight of the chain she spurned.
'Listen,' she cried. I heard a distant roar,
Like starving outcasts on a hungry shore,
Rise from a mighty city evermore.
And then anon, piercing that outer din,
Rose up the shriek of women mad with gin,
And hollow laugh of girls who sold their sin.
And as with age, gaunt on its mother's knee,
The babe cried out for bread, no bread had she;
Maddened she cursed her womb's fertility.
'Listen again!' She cried, and then hard by,
The rich man's music drowned that 'bitter cry,'
And harp and viol charmed the wintry sky.

    O Christ, eternal brother,
      Once more this day is thine;
    Once more to one another
      Our stony hearts incline!
    'Peace and goodwill?' And can it be
    That this is all we learnt of Thee:—

M

Who seemedst in those gracious years
To staunch the source of human tears;—
This splendour to despair allied,
A palace here, there, at its side,
Those dens of misery?
Oh! rather come the shocks that nations feel!
Come, Revolution, with the armèd heel!
Come Attila, with all thy Vandal crew!
Tread into dust our gold!
Respect not aught that's old!
Cast in a nobler mould   ·
Our state renew!
I turned, and looked to Truth, but Truth had fled;
Only there lingered on a voice, that said,
In solemn music, though in mournful tones,
Like wasted brook that murmurs o'er its stones,
Sad-echoing still:
'How little yet ye know the word
On that first dawn of Christmas heard,
The only power to right the wrong,
To fire the cold, and tame the strong,
To bring the pride of greatness down,
And mix the cottage with the crown,
The grand old glorious angel-song,
Peace and goodwill!'

Christmas, 1883.

IN THE BEGINNING.

AUGUST, year unknown; time, Six o'clock in the
    morning;
Sate in a tree an Ape; irrational; eating an apple,
Raw; no cook as yet, no house, no shred of a garment;
Soul, a blank; taste, nil; a thumb but slowly beginning;
Warranted wholly an Ape, a great Jack-ape of the forest,
Swinging with tail on bough; (O tail, oh! why have
    we lost it?
Better to swing on tail than Grace's skill at the
    wickets!)
Jabbering, hairy, grim, arboreal wholly in habits.
So he sate on till Noon, when, hushed in slumber
    around him,
Everything lay dead; all save the murmuring insect,
Whose small voice still spake, proclaiming silence.
    Awaking
Suddenly then he rose, and thinking scorn of his fellows
Longed to be quit of them, all, his Apess specially.
    She, dear,
Knew no dream, no vision; her Apelet playing about her
All her thought, her care! At Four, he finally left her,
Went to live by himself, but felt a pang—'twas a
    Conscience
Budding, in germ; yet went; then stopped to bathe in
    a fountain.
Wow! What an ugly phiz! He saw, and shuddered;
    a Ruskin
Stirred in his breast. Taste born!—the seed of a
    mighty Ideal,

M 2

Raffaelesque, Titianic! Erect he strode through the
    jungle,
Cleaving his way with a stick;—Art's rise! An imple-
    ment maker,
Parent of Armstrong guns, steam-rams, et cætera!
    Still on
Plucking the fruits he went; felt pain, no matter the
    region!
Said, it was not the apple, or crab, or cranberry; no! nor
Even the sloe; 'twas a chill. He caught it there in
    the fountain,
Bathing, still in a heat, the water cold o' the coldest.
Glorious Ape!—Logician! not yet a perfect Induction,
But good step that way, as good as many among us!
(Bacon not yet come, but coming a good time after,
Million years, or so! What's Time? A drop in the
    bucket.)
So he went on till Eve, when, reached the edge o' the
    forest,
Just where the opening paths sloped westward; then
    i' the gloaming,
Mounting a rising knoll, he saw the sun in his glory
Set over flood and fell; and joining, as in embraces,—
Like Ixion of old, the cloudland wedding the Titan,—
Earth to heaven draw near: he saw, and suddenly
    trembled;
Sudden his Apehood shrank as a robe, and fell from
    off him,
Like to the angel-wings that burst their chrysalis-casing;
Sudden a soul was born. He owned a Greater above
    him,
Near him, round him, in him, far away in the splendour,

Having a right to rule, and he a duty to serve It,
Way not always clear, but duty ever abiding.
And this happened at Eight, at Eight P.M. precisely
On that August day ; and, if you cannot believe it,
Go to your Darwin ; read, how an Ape grew man, and
    a moment,
Just one tick of the clock, though clocks not yet in-
    vented,
Was when his soul was not, another, his soul was
    quickened.
And this must be true, or else—unhappy dilemma—
Men and monkeys both have souls, or flourish without
    them.
So farewell, Ape-man ! Lo we, your progeny, greet you ;
Thank you much for a soul, and may we never forget it !

NOBODY AND SOMEBODY.

Nobody.

LEFT there, nobody's daughter,
    Child of disgrace and shame—
Nobody ever taught her
    A mother's sweet saving name :

Nobody ever caring
    Whether she stood or fell,
And men (are they men ?) ensnaring
    With the arts and the gold of Hell !

Stitching with ceaseless labour,
    To earn her pitiful bread ;
Begging a crust of a neighbour,
    And getting a curse instead !

All through the long hot summer,
　All through the cold dark time,
With fingers, that numb and number
　Grow white as the frost's white rime.

Nobody ever conceiving
　The throb of that warm young life,
Nobody ever believing
　The strain of that terrible strife!

Nobody kind words pouring
　In that orphan heart's sad ear;
But all of us, all, ignoring
　What lies at our door so near!

O sister! down in the alley,
　Pale, with the downcast eye,
Dark and drear is the valley,
　But the stars shine forth on high.

Nobody here may love thee,
　Or care if thou stand or fall;
But the great good God above thee,
　He knows, and He cares for all.

Somebody.

SOMEWHERE down in the meadows,
　Where the river and rivulet meet,
Watching the April shadows
　Over the hillside fleet.

Somebody bending near her,
   Noble in face and form;
And the Cross of the gallant wearer
   Was won in the battle's storm.

Somewhere at altar kneeling,
   Bride, with her maidens round;
While the great organ, pealing,
   Fills all the Abbey with sound:

Somebody's hand her's holding,
   Pledging a life for a life;
Somebody's arm enfolding,
   Calling her 'Wife, dear wife!'

Somewhere, in hall or garden,
   Mother and child, the Heir!
Nothing to fret or harden,
   Nothing to cause one care!

Love all her life caressing,
   Riches, a boundless store;
Crown upon crown of blessing!
   What can she ask for more?

O lady! on high uplifted,
   Lacking no earth-known thing,
Noble, and nobly-gifted,
   Yet has thy lot one sting:

This, that thy poor pale sister
   Pines in yon alley unseen;
And thou canst not assist her,
   Such is the gulf between.

TO AN OPTIMIST.

Dim eyes, clear-sighted only for the distance,
  Fond fancy poring on those hills of blue,
Blamest thou me, bent only on resistance
  To ills of nearer view?

You were a painter born, and I a fighter;
  You to love beauty, I to set wrong right;
You, where a thing is bright, to paint it brighter,
  I to say, 'Black's not white.'

Had you been saved of old when heaven's great ruin
  Crashed down in flood, and Hope itself looked dark,
You had admired 'the good that rain was doing,'
  And praised 'the accommodation of the Ark.'

You see but cherubs where, in misery bundled,
  Poor children rot unheeded in a mews;
You note the rainbow, where a mop is trundled
  With rinsings from the stews.

I have the fatal fault to see too clearly
  Blight in the bloom, and ill in all, to spy;
Believing truth itself is bought too dearly,
  If purchased with a lie.

So fail I, friend, to see earth as you see it,
  All sunshine, angels bursting from the blue;
Though with good health and money, I agree, it
  May, while they both last, do.

What then our difference? This! As cunning jugglers
  Who force the court-card, will not yield the plain,
You quote the one blest, not the hopeless strugglers,
  The millions in their pain.

I too see Good, but do not pause to praise it;
  Leave opiate praise, love rather tonic blame;
'Improveable' I hold the world; to raise it,
  Man's only lawful aim.

Yet, oh! thy pardon, Heaven, if oft-times grumbling
  I murmur o'er lost harvests' wasted toil:
I know it must be; yet it is so humbling,
  That best things soonest spoil.

CHRISTMAS, 1885.

CHRIST's star is bright, and yet our hearts are holden
  With dim forebodings, ghosts of gathering fear;
It is not as in days of childhood olden
  When Christmas seemed all cheer.

Then thought we not of India, Church, or Ireland,
  Of Parnell-followers, or of party-wiles;
But played at forfeits round the enchanted fireland,
  And, losing, paid in smiles.

A naughty child was then put in the corner:
  Ah! Mr. Speaker, could you put them now!
The shameless drone, the obstructive, and the scorner,
  With all the Irish row.

Life has moved onward, Grace is now a matron,
  Comely and prim, with children half-a-score;
While Jack of twenty charities is patron,
  M.P., and worse—a bore.

Things must move onward. 'All the world's a garden'
  (As some one said); fresh flowers old places fill;
And change must come, from Hatfield or from Hawarden,
  Think, say we, what we will.

So let it come, but temperate, not in fury,
  Not as from Birmingham our sages bawl;
But, like the wisdom of a British jury,
  Sober, and safe, and—small.

Then, slowly onward! 'Twill need cautious steering:
  Yet, statesmen, hating rashness, loathe delay!
Courage! in God's name forward, nothing fearing!
  England will follow if you lead the way.

And, O pale star of Christ the East adorning,
  Guide us, late wanderers, on to peace and rest!
Still through the night of time comes in the morning,
  And, though dark-shadowed, still the new is best.

ET QUI SIBI MORTEM.

I.

JUDGE not! 'Tis past thy ken;
  Strangely the web of destiny is ordered;
In highest-natured men
  The loftiest wit with depths of madness bordered.

Judge not! The taper's light
  Is too small measure for volcanoes burning;
This constant, feebly bright,
  That sudden, with wild flame, all barriers spurning.

Judge not! Beyond the grave
  We shall know better the immense great trial;
This man submits, a slave;
  The other fights, and dies, in fierce denial.

But he who views the strife
  Calm from without, more wise than those within it,
Counts the long 'Yes' of life,
  Not the one 'No,' the single faithless minute.

2.

One too many in life!
  And the ways of life grown dim!
So clear to the strong, who can hustle along,
  So tangled, and dark, to him!

One too many in life!
  And the places all seem filled:
No room for the wit that is feebly-lit!
  No place for the weakly-willed!

One too many in life!
  And the struggle must have an end;
For a body in pain may grow well again,
  But a broken heart how mend?

So, 'One too many in life!'
  And a sigh as he quits the scene:
And it is but a plunge, and Death's cold spunge
  Wipes out where his place hath been.

LIVE AND LET BE!

LIVE and let be! The Alpine heaven is bright,
  Tired cloudlets sleep along yon azure sea;
Soft airs steal by, and whisper, faint and light,
  Live and let be!

Live and let be! Is it not well to rest
  Sometimes from labour? live as do the flowers?
Bask in the sunshine? lie on Nature's breast,
  Not counting hours?

Not heeding aught, but on the pale worn cheek
  To feel the warm breath of the murmuring pine,
And watch on many a rose-flushed hoary peak
  Heaven's glory shine?

Is it not well? Sweet, too, at wondering eve
  To list the melody of tinkling bells,
And hear old echo in the distance weave
  Endless farewells!

Night, too, hath here her music deep and strong
  Of cataracts, solemn as an ancient psalm,
Whence the soul's fever, born in heat and throng,
  Grows cool and calm.

Live and let be! It will be time enough
  Hereafter to resume the great world's care,
When autumn skies are troubled, winds are rough,
  And trees are bare.

Then to renew the fight, the cause rewaken,
  Dare all the strife, the burden, and the pain,
Rally the weak; the downcast, the forsaken,
  Lift up again.

And what thou doest then, in Peace begotten,
　Shall show like Peace, her looks and tones recall,
And, all the frail and faulty Past forgotten,
　Bring good to all.

Till then let nothing past or future vex
　The untrammell'd soul, 'mid Nature's freedom free,
From thoughts that darken, questions that perplex,
　Live and let be!

THE SWALLOWS.

O MOTHER, will the swallows never come?
　Feel my cheek, 'tis hot and burning,
　And my heart is sick with yearning,
But I'm always well as soon as swallows come.

They brought me in a primrose yesterday:
　And when primroses are blowing,
　Then I know that winter's going;
And the swallows cannot then be far away.

Hark, my old thrush in the garden singing clear!
　How I love his note to follow!
　But the swallow, O the swallow,
Bringing summer with him, summer, is more dear.

And the lamb's bleat! could I see them once again,
　With their innocent sweet faces,
　And their friskings, and their races!
Once I used—but now I cannot stir from pain.

Mother, lift me, all this side is growing numb :
　Oh, how dark the room is! Fold me
　To your bosom, tighter hold me!
Or I shall be gone before the swallows come.

And the swallows came again across the wave ;
　And the sky was soft and tender,
　With a gleam of rainbow splendour,
As they laid their little darling in the grave.

And they often watch the swallows by her tomb ;
　And they strain to think, but straining
　Cannot still the heart's complaining ;
'She is better there where swallows never come.'

And they carved the bird she loved upon her stone ;
　Joyous guest of summer darting
　Hither, thither, then departing
In a night to joys of other worlds unknown.

LOSS AND GAIN.

Loss.

SOMETHING is gone :
　I know it by this pain :
But yesterday I had it ;
To-morrow, though I bade it,
　It would not come again.

Something is gone :
　What shall we that thing call?
A touch, a tone, that thrilled me
A hidden joy that filled me?
　Say that is all.

And now 'tis gone,
  Lightly as first it came;
The sky a little colder,
The heart a little older,
  All else the same.

All else the same?
  O death, all-covering sea,
Come with thy floods, and drown me!
That thing I sought to crown me
  Was all the world to me.

Angels look on:
  They too, as we, have striven:
It was not by despairing,
It was not by not caring,
  They conquered heaven.

Gain.

SOMETHING is come:
  I felt it yestereve:
The lark on high was singing,
The happy church-bells ringing;
  How could I grieve?

I could not grieve:
  An old man weary lay;
I lifted up his burden,
He blessed me, and in guerdon
  Mine slipped away.

It slipped away:
  There came a child in pain;
I soothed it, and soon after
A burst of April laughter
  Followed the rain.

How could I grieve?
  O blessed human heart!
That in the joy of giving
Hast found the bliss of living,
  Up, play thy part!

Strive, and not rest!
  Rest here below is none,
Beneath a sky o'erarching
The hosts of men are marching:
  Angels look on.

Yet not in dark,
  Nor wholly sad thy way;
But here in sunny meadows,
There overcast with shadows;
  So runs our day.

MELIORA PRIORA.

THERE sits a thrush in my garden,
  And sings on the topmost spray;
And its song is ever the loudest,
  In the hush at the close of day.

There lies a child in a bedroom,
  Whitegowned in a cot snow-white;
And her laugh is ever the gayest
  In the dusk, at the fall of night.

My beautiful child in her chamber,
  My beautiful bird on the tree,
Whence comes it, ye twin blithe spirits,
  Whence comes it, that burst of glee?

Is it thanks for the day just over,
  No stain in the Past to rue?
Or the joy of the living Present?
  Ah! would I could be like you!

Like you with a childlike nature
  (For the bird and the child are one),
Like you, on a joy remembered
  To sleep when the day is done!

In a moment the thrush has ended;
  In a moment the child lies down;
In a moment has sleep descended,
  And covered them both, God's own.

But I lie, and toss on my pillow;
  I lie there the whole night long;
And I hear the hour from the distant tower
  Toll forth like a doleful song.

Ah me, for the child's free spirit!
  Ah me, for the bird's gay tone!
Gifts greater we men inherit,
  But the light free heart has flown.

'EASY DOES IT.'

Do not hurry, do not flurry!
Nothing good is got by worry.
Bide the hour to make the spring!
Take life easy, that's the thing.

Do not trouble, do not trouble;
Heavy hearts make toiling double.
Groans the back with loaded pain?
Laugh, and 'twill grow light again.

N

Do not sorrow, do not sorrow!
Grief to-day is joy to-morrow.
Life flows smoothest after fears;
Eyes shine brightest washed with tears.

Hark the children, hark the voices!
Somewhere everything rejoices.
Blasts without of winter ring,
Yet inward mirth makes endless spring,

Soon from elms will rooks be cawing,
Young lambs leaping, old folk thawing:
Soon with a sunny April dawn
Will daisies bright bedeck the lawn.

Forward then to victory straining,
Forward as brave men uncomplaining!
Though cloud and tempest wrap the sky,
Yet wakes behind the Eternal eye,

Watching, wondering, yearning, knowing
Whence the stream, and where 'tis going.
Seems all mystery? By-and-by
He will speak, and tell us, Why.

IN ARCADY.

A LITTLE breath from spray to spray,
  That wanders with a purposed quiet,
As though it were so calm a day,
  To shock it were unholy riot.

A little cloudlet in the sky,
  That melts, and then its shape renewing,
Then melts again, as though on high
  'Twere holiday, and nothing doing;

A hum of bee, a little song
  Of bird in praise of endless summer,
That will not break the stillness long,
  But leaves it to a chance new-comer;

A little sound of rippling stream
  Now heard, now hushed, its deep leaves under;
Like murmurs of an infant's dream
  That barely part sweet lips asunder;

And Ocean's face for many a mile
  In calm, with scarce a wavelet breaking,
As sleeping eyelids ope awhile,
  Then close again without awaking;—

All say 'tis noon, and Silence sleeps
  With Beauty. Hence, and leave her sleeping,
Lulled by the tiny fall that leaps
  Beside her there in silver leaping.

Noon in the South! a perfect thing
  Of love, and light, and warmth, and colour
That, drowsy as a vampire's wing,
  Float round the soul in sloth to lull her.

Noon in the South! Then haste, away,
  Dear Soul, away, we may not tarry!
Enough, if hence for many a day
  Some sunshine of the heart we carry.

Enough, if 'mid our mist, and snow,
  We may in darker hours remember, ·
The bliss, the warmth, the southern glow,
  That mingled July with December.

But now a harp of loftier tone
  I hear resound to Dorian measure,
Say, Arcady is rest alone,
  But toil is strung to nobler pleasure.

Say, Arcady is fair and fine,
  Where Pan is lord of Man and Nature;
But 'neath his face and form divine
  Lurks cloven hoof of Faun and Satyr.

And sadness sits in every eye,
  And cynic youth is old at twenty;
Who looks for aught in Arcady
  But languid ease and '*far niente*'?

Then hence away, and Northward ho!
  Where souls and limbs of men are stronger:
But, O ye powers of frost and snow,
  Would holidays were somewhat longer!

A SPRIG OF HOLLY.

I FOUND it, a sprig of holly,
  It had fallen from an unknown hand,
In the home of the pine and myrtle,
  Far off in this Southern land.

And I know not whose hand had cast it,
  Or careless, or rude with scorn,
Whether pleased with a brighter berry,
  Or pricked with its guard of thorn.

But there it lay in the pathway,
  Poor sprig with its berries three,
Like a waif or a stray from England,
  And it seemed a message to me.

Then sudden there flashed a vision
  Of a Christmas far away;
Of a firelight shed on a curtain red,
  And the shouts of the children at play.

And a fir-tree shone in the centre,
  And around it a wondering ring,
Where the Snow-King kisses the Fairy,
  And the Fairy frowns at the King.

And the dances! the valse! the polka!
  And Sir Roger must wait his turn;
For, with breath all a-flame, the great Snapdragon came,
  And how blue all the tapers burn!

And awe is on childish faces,
  And as in all things below,
You must first begin, if you wish to win,
  To suffer; a fact we know.

So the Snow-King puffs at his fingers,
  And the Fairy pities his pain,
And, had he now kissed her instead of his blister,
  She would not have frowned again.

And so through the long, bright evening,
  Until all the games are played,
And child-vows given (smile on them, Heaven!)
  Forgotten as soon as made.

For there must be kissing and cooing
  Of birds in the nest at play,
As there must be wedding and wooing
  Of birds full grown, some day.

And little Alice is sleeping,
  Wide-mouthed in a wide arm-chair,
One fat round arm fast keeping
  That idol with flaxen hair.

When—hark! Is it 'ten' there striking?
  And look! Do the lights burn low?
Then sudden is heard the terrible word,
  Away! it is time to go.

And I started, and lo! the holly
  Lay bright in the pathway there,
With the dark-hued sheen of its prickly green
  Guarding its fruitage fair.

And I love it, my sprig of holly,
  Though it boast but its berries three ;
For whatever it seem to others,
  It was surely a message to me.

And dear as the mountains round me,
  And dells where the waters run,
And the peaks and pines, where for ever shines
  The glow of a summer sun.

No mist in the soft-toned valley,
  No wind in the unstirred tree,
No stain on the cloudless ether,
  No wave on the breathless sea!

Yet dearer to me that vision
  Of home, and of Christmas bells!
And it came to me all at the holly's call,
  In the heart of the Esterelles.

SONNETS.

TOUJOURS DE L'AUDACE.

ONCE in our lives we know what men we are :
In common hours we live as common men,
Our valour not true valour; and a star
Shines not more distant than our Now, and Then.
Anon, as winds that shake a stagnant deep,
Comes there awakening. On some glorious day
Dull custom drops from off us like a sleep,
And fear, a horrid nightmare, slinks away :
And we are free, and freedom is a power
Of joy, of inspiration, Only dare,
Dare strongly! When it comes, the day, the hour,
Delay not! Coming dangers throng the air :
Before us lie the paths of light or gloom,
Λ greater England, or decay and doom.

Ναὶ μὰ τούς.

WHEN the Athenian orator of yore
Would lift his country to its earlier height,
By Marathon and Salamis he swore,
And pointed to their glories, full in sight.
So by Trafalgar, and by Waterloo,
Let us too swear, we will not yield one inch
For sloth, or weakness. We have work to do
Greater with greater empire. Shall we flinch
Degenerate? Nay, with strong embattled host
Hold we our land, with fleets our subject seas!
Mistrust the very breakers round our coast,
Lest they be leagued to admit our enemies!
We have in us the blood of Nelson's men :
Has it grown cold? 'Twas liquid lava then.

'HE PURGETH IT.'

NATIONS need sometime suffering: when our mood
Is soft, emasculate, and fearing pain;
When indolence and torpor chill the blood,
And insolence and bluster fire the brain;
When, puny sons of mighty sires, we deem
Our father's stature greater than our own,
We cannot wear their armour, and we dream
Heroic dreams, the life heroic flown:
Then oh! come loss, come suffering—only shame
Be absent! come, and to our souls discover,
Ere the reluctant day of grace be over,
Lost manhood's greatness, now inert and tame!
Virtue's foundation strong is to be bold;
The nobler metal iron is, not gold.

A YEAR OF SILENCE.

OH, for a year of silence! Could we go
Each to our quiet desk, or house, or field,
And cease our babbling; plough, and reap, and sow;
And read old books, and ransack treasure sealed
Of learning, writ in ages long ago!
Then let some strong-souled Gordon take the field
Of action; while the masters, 'they who know,'
Would ravage Time, its honeyed stores to yield!
That were as dreamland! Pulpit, senate, mart,
Suddenly silent; only nature heard
With her still music, or her prophet's word!
The while the noisy blusterer would depart
Where men talk least, his year of grace to spend,
To learn his ignorance and his manners mend!

('In some of the United States, the local Congress does not
meet every year.'—*Bryce.*)

SORROW.

Sorrow came to him with a pleading face;
He would not rise and bid her enter in;
She seemed to claim in him too large a space,
And he was careless, full of mirth and sin:
So passed she onward. Then it chanced one day,
When Autumn winds in woods were making moan,
Again did gentle Sorrow fare that way,
And heard him mourning, for his love had flown.
So once again she sought him. Reckless, rude,
He bade her enter. Then with stately mien,
She came, she took possession like a queen,
And seemed not sorrow, but a joy subdued;
Bringing a shadow, yet, as shadows are,
A blessing cast from some great Light afar.

SWEET SORROW.

Who hath not loved her who hath ever tried her?
Who doth not owe her more of joy than tears?
Who doth not grudge the hours he hath denied her,
The careless hours, the laughter-loving years?
Who doth not know his life more worth the living,
Now she hath blessed it; now her teacher Pain
Hath purged his vision, and with gracious giving
Restored it cleansed to purer sight again?
Sorrow, sweet Sorrow! Now at length 'tis over,
The storm, the fret, the fever—and 'tis well,
Well, if within we can our good discover
In peace; we thought it once in strife to dwell,
In storm, in fret, in fever. But 'tis past:
The battered swimmer finds sure ground at last.

A SONG OF BATTLE.

CHARGE, bayonets, charge! but gently, not too wildly!
　For fear they 'buckle in,' prod not too hard!
Out, sabres, out! But, mind you, use them mildly!
　Perhaps they're safer only kept on guard.

Hold your revolvers ready! If some barrels
　(Say two or three) should not discharge their ball,
There 'll be some Arabs left for future quarrels,
　A generous army would not kill them all.

On, then, remembering that your arms are brittle!
　'England expects' her soldiers not to waste:
For though, 'tis true, they cost the country little,
　Yet, if they're broken, they must be replaced.

On, then, brave Atkins, stalwart, strong and fiery!
　Whoever blunders, you are always game:
And then a Parliamentary inquiry
　Will show, some years hence, who it was to blame.

RELIGIO ACADEMICI.

I.

WHAT, you have found Him not in the world-wide dome
　　of St. Peter's,
　Not in the cross-crowned height, not in the Cata-
　　combs' cell?
Not in Ravenna mosaic, or air-built glory of Milan?
　Not in the sun-flushed Alp, rose of the morning, afar?
'Ah! not there! Then eastward! Away, where mys-
　　tery lingers,
　Far over ancient waves on to the home of the sun!

Borne upon ardent feet with the eager heart of the
    pilgrim,
  There to the garden of God, there to the cradle of all!
Surely, He must be there. On high, lo! Sinai thunders
  Lonely and awful, bare, save for the cloud on its brow.
Surely I there must find Him; His voice shall speak,
    and His footprints
  Start from the furrowy rock, shine on the billowy sand.
Still not there! still hidden! nor where, with dearer
    devotion,
  Memory tracks the scene Saints and Apostles have
    trod;
Not on Jerusalem heights, nor where Gethsemane
    slumbers,
  Shadowy, mystic, pale, lit with the Passover moon.
Vain, all vain! I found not. A dream He floated be-
    fore me,
  Nearer by night; with dawn, ghostly, He faded away.
Gone! and to worldly eyes in the shrine of His earthly
    abiding
  Galilee was but a lake; Nazareth only a name.
Only a name! and nothing availed it to waken the
    echoes,
  There where the Holiest dwelt, reading the story
    divine.
Beauty may linger still on the snow-capped summit of
    Hermon,
  Beauty, a life-giving stream, creep over valley and
    plain;
Beauty may shine in the lily, or blush in the dark
    oleander;
  Bethlehem maids go by smiling and sweet as of yore;

But the old faith was gone : the sky hung brazen above
     me,
  Empty and blank : hope dead : Deity gone from it all.
Gone as a vision of light when a dreamer wakes, or a
     phantom
  Seen in the clouds, our own image reflected afar.
Gone ; nothing left but Beauty! in Dresden gallery
     roaming
     Still may I stand, still gaze rapt on Madonna and
     Child :
Still with the wondering crowd in the gorgeous Vatican
     chamber
     Draw a deep breath, as I watch Christ, the Trans-
     figured, on high ;
Still in the spiritual world, in the cloudland region of
     fancy,
     Joy, as I see great shapes, ghosts of the Future, go by :
Still with an open heart, in the grand Pantheon of
     Nature,
     Hymn the great mystery, kneel as to a Goddess su-
     preme.
Still, with Beethoven, thrill as the storm-tost passion of
     music
     Sinks like a wildered dove to a Nirvana of rest :
Nothing remains but Beauty.' He said, and wearily
     sighing,
     Sat upon Shotover stile, gazing on Oxford below,
Minaret-crowned St. Mary's, and Magdalen Tower, and
     Merton,
     Far-off jewels of light, fringed with a circle of shade,
Set in the shining floods. Oh! not alone in the sun-
     shine

Fair ! yet fairer the faith, glory of men who believed,
Mother of noble works, which built them there in the
    foretime,
    Dreaming of God; then woke, strong to a labour
    divine.
Strong with a magical skill, a noble army of builders,
    Early afoot, with prayer carving their vision in stone,
Flower of the field, and lily, and leaf, and traceried
    window,
    Endless vanishing lines, as when a forest is bare !
As when a forest is clothed, that arch ! that forest of
    arches,
    Mystical, echoing ! Hark ! Music of angels is there,
Melody Magdalen-chanted; afar it rose in the distance,
    Bringing a prayer to the lip, bringing a tear to the eye,
Borne on the breeze, or fancied. We sate. The city
    illumined
    Shone as a rose : night-shades slowly beginning to fall.
Ah, what a vision was there ! But then a vapour as-
    cending
    Rose over turret and spire, crept over College, and
    Hall,
Death-white, all-enfolding. As when from marshy
    Maremna,
    Rises a poisonous breath, ghastly—inhale it, and die !
' Look ! that is me,' he whispered, ' I had it once, I am
    certain,
    Once I had faith. But now ! Now there is mist
    over all.'

II.

What? You have nowhere found Him? And I, I see
     Him around me
  Everywhere; here first, throned in the spirit of Man.
Not in the rushing of worlds, or the timeless passage
     of ages;
  Not in the sunbuilt arch; not in the cataract's roar;
Not in the mightiest wing that soars o'er the summit
     of Andes;
  Not in the tiniest life born in a drop of the sea;
But in the human spirit! O Man, imperial Master,
  Swifter than light thought-borne through the great
     Ocean on high,
Tracking a sunbeam here, and there with balance
     gigantic
  Holding a star in thy hand, puny but weighing a
     world:
' Know thyself,' yet greater than all thy vision beholdeth!
  Wonderful all, yet thou wonderful even beyond!
Hark! 'Tis His voice; thou hear'st Him. A God is
     speaking within thee;
  Terrible now it commands; Sinai thunders within;
' This thou shalt, thou shalt not.' Anon, as after the
     thunder
  Follows a gentle rain, soft with the piping of birds,
So in the calm still bosom is heard the cry of a Father—
  Tenderly now it approves,—' Son, be thou ever with
     me!
Bring him the new best robe, the signet-ring of the
     Master!
  Slavery's every badge washed, with dishonour, away!

Sing him the new great song of the Father's love!'
   And the Angels
Hymning a new-born soul, jubilant sang it on high.
'Beautiful! Here is beauty, above the hue of the rain-
   bow:
Majesty stern, but sweet: Father and Mother in one.
Rainbow-promise is good; but home-lit beacon is better,
   Over the lurid waves lighting the mariner home.'

  .   .   .   .

And thou hast loved her, Beauty? Thou doest well!
   'Tis a maiden
   Fairer than words; her smile drawn from the bosom
     of Love.
Guard her, and let no touch of the beast or Satyr
   assail her;
   Honour her; hear from her lips, ponder her story
     divine!
Who, when the morning stars in the bridal joy of
   Creation
   Shouted her birth, came forth loveliest daughter of God;
Came and to cheer men's souls, with the brake and
   briar contending,
   Gave to the thistle a bloom, budded a rose on the
     thorn;
Flowers in her track sprang up as she passed, and
   winds of the woodland
   Sighed into melody: man heard, and his spirit grew
     mild.
Fair is she, fairer than all. But shall her Beauty en-
   snare thee
   Slave to her smile, love-bound, yearning for nothing
     beyond?

Dreamer, content with a dream, and the sunlit wall of
 a dungeon
  Deeming a palace? A cell, seeming a kingdom to
   thee?
Nay but, O man, look upward! Her hand shall lift
 thee, and lead thee
  Up to the home of her birth, back to her Father
   and Thine,
Up through the burnished clouds, and the flaming
 track of the sunset;
  Up through the golden stars, gleam of a glory beyond;
World flashing light to world as they pass, like ships
 in the darkness
  Showing a light, then soon dash into darkness again.
Up through the endless spaces, expansion after expan-
 sion;
  Up to the great white throne; up to the presence
   of God!
There shall she fold her wing, and, all her mission
 accomplished,
  Join with the spirits on high, singing to ravish the
   spheres:
'Glory to God in the highest.' The lifelong struggle is
 over;
  Over, the fire and the fret; over, the rack and the pain;
Failure of hope; love's discord! The joy that ended
 in madness,
  Over at last! Life closed, like its beginning, in tears!
Mystery all, for God was the cause. But Love in the
 distance,
  Holding an amaranth crown, Love was the goal of
   it all.

III.

' Love ! He is love ! ' I said it, where endless smoke, as
  a furnace,
  Hangs o'er the Dead-sea wave, grave of Gomorrah
  of yore;
There where the bale-fire fell, and the dark sulphur-
  eous waters,
  Closing above as a pall, hid the abhorrèd of God.
' Love ! He is love ! ' I said it, where old Vesuvius thun-
  ders,
  Still with the fire in his heart, still with the wrath
  on his brow;
There where the gay bright cities of fair Parthenope's
  girdle
  Trembled, as out of the cloud slowly the horror
  came down;
Trembled, and when light dawned they knew that a
  judgment had fallen :
  Two of their number were not; two of the circle
  had gone.
' Gone ! Was it love to slay them, the gay, the bright
  in the foretime,
  When the young earth yet knew barely the good
  and the ill ?
When as an insect-race men wantoned gay in the
  sunshine,
  Fiercer the fire in the breast, hotter the blood in the
  vein ?
Hard, where the rose twice blossoms to seek austerity's
  winter !
  Hard, to exact life's frost there in the land of the
  Sun ! '

o

Nay, it was love, I answered. The keenest knife is
    the kindest,
  Where the whole body is sick, stern to dissever a
    limb ;
Stern, where the poison works, and the cureless, can-
    cerous ulcer
Threatens the life, forthwith ruthless to lop it away.
Canaan's profitless tribes, corrupt Assyrian greatness,
  Roman, Egyptian, Greek, rotten they perish in
    turn ;
City, or prince, or people, what do ye sinning against
    Him ?
  Here on His earth, God's work thwarting His pur-
    pose to man ?
Stern is the warrior's sword when a foe is writhing
    beneath him ;
Justice is stern : but Love, love is the sternest of all ;
Love is too great for pity. A moan is heard on the
    mountains ;—
  Infinite dirge—one race dying is passing away :
Life for a moment passes : the stream is slack at the
    fountain :
  Earth, as a breast grown old, cannot its sources
    supply :
Listless the people sit ; and the womb is barren, the
    altar
  Cold ; and a shuddering race creep to their caverns
    and die ;
Die, and bequeath but an echo that haunts that cavern-
    ous chamber,
  'Ours was the Paradise once : lost, it is never re-
    gained.'

Only a pause! Life's winter! A glacial age! And a
    seed-time
Big with humanity's hope pointing to better beyond!
Only a pause! Then Nature awakes, and—torrent gi-
    gantic—
Fresh with Niagara force rushes again to the sea.
Love is too great for pity. He loved them, e'en when
    he smote them;
    But love is stern. Elsewhere planted the wicked
      may mend;
Broken the evil trammel, the bad tradition of elders,
    Lust as a poisonous dream passed with the body
      away:
Or, as a sixth strong sense, millenniums' horror of evil
    Burnt in the soul, so long separate living from God.
Mystery all! We know not. We shoot a shaft at a
    venture
Into the void. Perchance there we may find it again:
It, or a something better, or something different wholly:
    Leave it to Love. With Love there we shall find it
      again.
And meanwhile this faith I hold, and carry about me,
    Small as a taper's spark lighting the infinite gloom:
What is good for the whole will be also good for the
    unit:
    Law is beneficent love: love is benevolent law.
Vast is the whole wide world, but Love enfolding it
    vaster:
    Leave it to Love! Outside Love there is nothing
      at all.
'And what of me,' he murmured, my friend with the
    delicate features,

Over his sad, worn face flitting a shadow of scorn,
'Me, to whom life is dreary, and faith is dark, and the
    problem
    Higher than Teneriffe's height, deeper than Africa's
        sand;
If He but care for the many, the good of the general
    ant-hill,
    Not for the separate ant drawing its separate load;
If I, a millionth, get but a millionth part of a millionth
    Fraction of love, then what—what is this blessing to
        me?'

.

AMMERGAU.

WE shrink to bare Him to the light intense
Of hard-eyed cavil, in the glare of day:
His agony we act not to the sense,
Lest human grief the Godhead should betray,
And lower Him to the level of our clay.
And we do well. But they who have not soared
So high, to know alone a risen Lord,
Nor sunk so low to let Him. fade away
Into a cold abstraction—they do well,
They too, these peasants in their pastures green,
Still in their Alpine solitude to tell
The awful tale; still o'er His Passion's scene
To weep; then, grieving o'er their dear Lord's pain,
Go forth resolved never to sin again.

PEACE.

WINDS and wild waves in headlong huge commotion
  Scud, dark with tempest, o'er the Atlantic's breast :
While, underneath, few fathoms deep in Ocean,
  Lie peace, and rest.

Storms in mid-air, the rack before them sweeping,
  Hurry, and hiss, like furies hate-possessed:
While, over all, white cloudlets pure are sleeping
  In peace, in rest.

Heart, O wild heart ! why, in the storm-world ranging,
  Flit'st thou thus midway, passion's slave and jest,
When, all so near, above, below, unchanging
  Are heaven, and rest ?

HEAVEN.

CLOUD, and still cloud, o'erhanging sombre, livid,
  They crush the soul with anguished, mute despair:
Yet one far hill in sunshine, clear and vivid,
  Says, Heaven is there.

An inky sky above an inky ocean,
  Wild seabirds screaming down the startled air:
Yet one bright islet, calm amid commotion,
  Says, Heaven is there.

So bright, so calm, my soul, from Nature borrow
  Her secret, always calm and bright somewhere ;
And one serener spot, defying sorrow,
  Keep ! Heaven is there.

JOY AND GRIEF.

He sang of joy,
　It had a ring of pain;
He sang of grief,
　It was the sweeter strain.

For pain is brief,
　And, ere the pain is old,
Comes joy's relief;
　The worst is never told.

And joy is brief,
　And, while the joy is young,
There enters grief;
　The best is never sung.

The best is never sung,
　The worst is never told;
What harp was ever strung
　Could passion's depth unfold?

Passion, whose glowing springs
　Burn with so fierce a fire,
'Twould burst the poet's strings,
　And shrivel up his lyre.

SHADOWS.

Shadows of the morning, on the way,
Shadows of a morning, fresh and gay,
　Shadows of the morning, like a maiden's tears
　　adorning
For her bridal, Oh! how soon ye pass away!

Shadows of the noontide, cool and calm,
Shadows of oasis, and of palm,
  Where a weary pair are resting, after heat of desert
    blest in
Airs that wander in those shadows, breathing balm!

Shadows of the evening, how they fall
Sombre, dank, and heavy, like a pall!
  Slow at first they quicken, then they thicken, thicken,
    thicken,
Till they rush upon us, myriads, veiling all.

Shadows of the midnight, dark and drear,
Shadows of the midnight, fraught with fear;
  But for hopes we fondest cherish, faiths we dare not
    let to perish,
O ye awful, awful, shadows! And, how near!

OUR CHILDREN.

I LOOKED at the happy children
  Who gathered around the hearth;
So blithe they were, no children
  Could happier be on earth;
With their merry plays, and their winsome ways,
  And the sound of their silvery mirth!

Then I thought of those other children,
  So wizened, and hard, and bold,
Who huddle in slum and cellar,
  And shiver with want and cold:
Not fresh as the dew, or the morning's hue,
  But haggard, and lean, and old.

But yet may they still, those children,
  Be taught to forget their pain ;
And, gathered in arms that love them,
  Their laughter may come again ;
And the stare of woe, and the craft may go,
  And the bosom be washed of stain.

But it is not in cold book learning
  Those children's hearts to move :
And the Spirit to stir their spirit
  Must come from the realms above ;
'Tis an angel alone can touch them,
  And that angel's name is Love.

For whatever the world may fancy,
  And whatever the wise men say
Of our nineteenth-century progress,
  Of a new and a better way :
Still it takes a soul to make a soul
  Now as in the olden day.

AFTER HORACE.

MARCH.

LITTLE buds of greenness
  Bursting from the ground ;
Blasts of icy keenness
  Withering all around ;

Thrush and blackbird singing
  On the reddening larch ;
Sleet and hailstorm slinging
  Down the winds of March ;

Thus they live together
　Like a stormy mind,
Bright and bitter weather
　In one month combined;

Here a sunny hour
　Glinting through the grey,
There a golden flower
　Struggling into day;

Gleams of growing kindness
　In a melting sky,
Then with utter blindness
　Snowdrifts sweeping by.

So, with bud and blossom,
　Softer, sweeter air,
In Neæra's bosom
　Find I my despair.

For while wood birds warble,
　And winds change their tone,
She unmoved as marble
　Stately stands, alone.

She than moonlight colder
　Keeps her wintry sky,
Freezing the beholder
　With ungentle eye;

Lovely onward gliding,
　But, imperfect whole,
Loveless still abiding,
　Unawaked the soul.

APRIL.

It was a flower, a little flower,
  Of simple blue and gold,
A maiden sowed it, a gardener hoed it
  We watched the flower unfold.

There came one day a lover gay,
  The maiden's look was shy;
He plucked the flower in careless hour,
  And said, I will her try.

He gave it to her, that careless wooer,
  She did not turn away;
By sun and moon, and all that's soon,
  She was his own that day.

MAY.

We had a flower, a little flower,
  We lived for it alone;
One daughter fair of beauty rare,
  We thought her all our own.

So passed the hour of sun and shower,
  Till April bloomed to May;
Then came another, and father, mother,
  Were naught: she has flown away.

OCTOBER.

It was the time of Autumn,
  When leaves were turning brown,
Green to yellow, and pied, and black,
  And some were tumbling down.

It was the time of Autumn,
  When fruits are gathered in,
Some for the press, and some for the vat,
  And some for the miller's bin.

Then poor folk fell a-singing,
  Because their work was o'er;
And rich folk fell a-sighing,
  That they could play no more.

For the summer-time is a merry time,
  If a man have leisure to play;
But the summer-time is a weary time,
  If a man must work alway.

And a cloud sits on the mountain,
  And a mist lies in the vale;
And the moon swims, and vapour dims
  Her horn; and the sun is pale.

And love, who dwells in summer skies,
  And droops, when they are not,
Departed, as the swallow flies,
  Forgetting, and forgot.

DECEMBER .

It was but the wild waves playing,
  It was but the wild wind's roar,
It was but a pale maid straying
  Alone by a wreck-strewn shore.

It was but a day of December
  That followed a day of June;
But to spirits that can remember,
  What a wail in the words, "'Tis done'!

The dream is broken and faded,
　　The joy departed and flown;
And to bosoms that loved as they did
　　'Tis death to live on alone.

O sea, that her lover art hiding,
　　O wind, with the dirge-like tune,
There's a fathomless gulph dividing
　　A day of December and June.

IDEM.

HE stepped from the darkened chamber,
　　He passed to the cold white air,
And he knew that the world's best treasure
　　Lay buried behind him there.

For it was not an idle fancy,
　　Nor a foolish boy's light whim,
Nor the love of a heart that is touched in part;
　　It was all the world to him.

And perhaps it will take him one year,
　　Perhaps it will take him two,
Perhaps he will never forget it,
　　As some poor creatures do,

Perhaps it will live for ever,
　　Engrained in his memory,
And be heard as a sigh in the songs on high
　　Of the blest by the crystal sea.

HODGE.

ON SAVING.

WHAT 's the use o' savin', when there 's nowt for a man
to buy ?
Cow, and cottage, and garden, that 's not for the like o' I.
Land ! that 's for they big 'uns as live up there on the
hill ;
Not for low-born fellers, like you, and me, and Bill.

> Then drink, boys ; drink, boys ; never stop to think,
> boys ;
> Wi' wages high let money fly ;
> To-morrow they may sink, boys.

What 's the use o' savin', when they help yer if ye
are ill,
Four bob every week, Jimmy, and pay your Doctor's
bill ?
There 's some as abuse them Guardians, and say they 're
hard as a stone,
But folk come to like 'em better, Jimmy, better the
more they 're known.

> Then drink, &c.

What 's the use o' savin', wi' Parson close at the door,
And allays soup in his kitchen, and he so good to the
poor ?
And a reglar lady up yonder, wi' a sight o' money and
land,
And cold meat had for the asking, and the purse never
out o' her hand.

> Then drink, &c.

What's the use o' savin', when there's allays grub to
    be had,
Skilly at night and morning, and the stuff is none so
    bad ?
And so, if yer like a tramp, Jimmy, yer can pass from
    ward to ward,
Only a little oakum to pick, and that's not hard.

       Then drink, &c.

What's the use o' savin', o' putting away your cash,
And just when yer want your money, your club is sure
    to smash?
Fuddle, and fuddle, and fuddle, up there at the Royal
    Oak,
That's how your managers manage, and so the club
    gets broke.

       Then drink, &c.

What's the use o' savin', when yer 've ollers 'the House'
    at last,
'Poor Man's Home' they call it, when strength and
    health are past?
They say, yer lose your good name, if once them walls
    yer see ;
But, lor ! good name's for rich folk, Jimmy ; it's not for
    the like o' we.

       Then drink, &c.

Then what's the use o' savin', and they bury yer, too,
    when dead ;
Coffin o' deal, that's all ; but who wants a coffin o' lead?

So yer cannot be better for savin', and yer cannot be
    worse if yer spend,
And it's jolly o' nights to sit here, Jimmy, and drain
    a glass wi' a frend.

    Then drink, &c.

1874 (about).

ON CHURCH-GOING.

I DOAN'T go to Church, 'cause I cannot see the good ;
And yet I'm none so sartin I should go there if I could ;
For I does what I likes, and jest when I likes, d'yer see?
And I've none so great a liking for them there seats
    'called Free.'

I doan't go to Church, 'cause my coat is getting old,
And the big folks look and mutter, 'Beggars, sure, is
    getting bold.'
Mebbe, some day up in heaven, if they get there, they
    will larn,
Them above don't stop to ask yer if your coat has got
    a darn.

I doan't go to Church, cause the place it be so grand,
Fit for them with coach and 'osses, wi' great housen,
    and wi' land ;
And then Parson he's so larned, what a' means I can-
    not tell ;
Folks speaks plainer down at Chappul. How they du
    go on at Hell!

I doan't go to Church, cause, wi' Squoire a' sitting there,
I keep thinking what he called me, when he cotched
    me wi' a snare;
It wer jest outside my garden, yet the names that he
    did call!
Thief and poacher! lawkamussy! but a rabbut arter
    all!

Parson, he's a kind old gem'man, and his wife is kinder
    still,
Wi' her trac's, and wi' her pudden, and her bottles when
    ye're ill;
But it's not what I wants, to be tinkered when I'm
    down;
It's to get up, and to keep up, and 'ave summat o' my
    own.

That's the thing. And if the Boible (as them farmers
    du agree)
Be agen poor folk a' rising, then I'll let the Boible be.
Parson says, I'm but a haythen. Well, a toad 'ull love
    his hole.
If he cared more for my body, p'raps I'd care more
    for my soul.

So I doan't go to Church, 'cause I dunnot see the good;
But I takes a walk instead of 't in the holler by the
    wood;
And my dawg he goes behind me, and I smoakes all
    the way;
He's a rare 'un still at rabbuts, is my old dawg Tray.

    1875 (about).

VOX VENTURA.

Wʜᴀᴛ 'll I do with my vote, when I 've got it? Nay,
    don't yer ask!
Tapping your beer 's no good, till yer 've got your beer
    in the cask;
Votin' agen my Squoire sounds all very moity and
    grand,
But I 'll not talk o' my vote till I 've got my vote i'
    my hand.

Harkee, however, my frend! Ye 're makin' a speech
    yer say:
' Got to get up your case.' Well! can keep a secret? Aye?
Then look here! ' Sit down! A pipe, and a pottle o' ale?'
Well, doan't mind if I do. Here 's to yer? And now,
    my tale!

Fust, my house! As I am, a pig fares better nor I,
Feeds as well, doan't work, and lives in a fust-rate stye.
We 've one room for all. And with that, there 's none
    as can
Bring up a family dasent; no, not if he 's twoice a man.

Then my garden! See, I 'd like it just twoice as big;
Handy when work is slack, and room enough for a pig;
' Muck is money,' yer know, and then a pig 'll eat
What yer cannot, or won't, and he turns it all to meat.

Then, my childern! Bob, and Sal, and ten of 'em more;
Like enough they seem, please Heaven, to reach a score;
Parson says, I mun pay their schoolin'; but I doan't see
Why I should pay a penny; why can't yer teach 'em free?

Then there's a cow, an' grass. The young 'uns look thin
    an' pale;
Wife, she says it's the want o' milk, it's dearer nor ale :
Farmers send theirs to Lunnon, o' coorse they do;
    it pays :
So, I'll go for a cow, an' a acre o' land, to graze.

Politics? Well, see here! I were ollers loyal an' true,
An' when beer were plenty my colours were allers
    'Blue';
Fought for it, too, like a man ; an' I made the old town
    ring
Hollering Church an' State, an' all that sort o' thing.

Jim, he voted 'Yeller,' an' talked o' cheapenin' bread;
Radical chap were Jim ; 'ow I used to punch 'is 'ead !
But, when I've got a vote, can't say but p'raps I'll go
An' vote along wi' Jim. Yer must move with the times,
    yer know.

Work? Nay, I doan't mind workin', as long as it ain't
    too hard.
Wages? I doan't want nothin' as isn't a fair reward.
But my idee and the farmers' they doan't agree alway;
They want yer to work twelve hours, an' get two shillin'.
    a day.

No, Sir! That won't do! A slave is a slave, an' lives
Just where his master tells him, an' takes what his
    master gives ;
But, when I've a vote, I'll show 'em—I'll let my
    master see—
If he do nothing for I, then I'll—But let that be !

Time for more? Well then, when a man's grown old,
    an' past
Work, I say it's a shame he should go to 'the House'
    at last;
Tied up there like a dog, an' never go out unless
Master gives yer leave, and then in a pauper dress!

Sir, I'm an English-man, d'ye hear? an' I'd just as lief
Go to H-ll as 'the House'; so I'll have out-door relief;
Four an' sixpence a week, an' a loaf a day, an' a ton
O' the best o' coal at Christmas—an' more when that
    is done.

There, now yer've got it all; but doan't yer say it's
    fro' me:
Squoire, he doan't like folk as speaks their mind too
    free;
Now I mun stand wi' my hat in my hand, as he
    goes by:
P'raps there's some as 'll stand wi' their hat to me, by
    an' bye.

   1883.

VOTING BY BALLOT.

There's Mister Bull down in these parts, an' a fine old
    gent he weer,
An' he's sarved in hevery Parlament for wellnigh thirty
    year;
An' there's Simon Brown, 'is gardener, as lives i' the
    lodge hard by,
An' a ticklish chap is Simon, as they say he's horful
    sly.

Then sez Mister Bull to Simon, 'Look 'ere, my frend,'
    sez he,
'Ther's the great Elekshun cummin' on, an' a fearful
    fight ther'll be :
An' ther's sum as wants new heverything, an' the Church
    an' Queen 'ull fall,
An' the rates 'ull be tremenjous, Simon, and they'll turn
    me out o' the Hall.

'An' ther's Gladstun, an' Joe Chamberlen; an', true as
    yer name is Brown,
If them two gets the hupper 'and, this country 'll shure
    go down;
An' the tother side ther's Salsbury, an' Lord Randy,
    our new star ;
An' I wish that young man 'ad more sense, as he's too
    much cheek by far.

'But them's the men to stick to, Simon, as puts no tax
    on beer :
An' as got no maggits in ther 'ead, an' the right sow
    by the ear :
An' them's the men to drive the coach, an' put on curb
    an' drag,
An' stan' no himperent Rooshan lies, no caperin' French-
    man's brag.

'Now, I wants to know this of yer, as 'as ate my bred
    so long,
An' the missus as gives yer childern clothes, an fisic
    to make 'em strong;
An' the ballot-box be hanged, Simon, as lets nun know
    who's who ;
An' how do yer mean to vote, my lad? Say out, is't
    yeller or blue ?'

Then that ole man he look'd hup an' down, an' 'is smile
  cum strange an' queer,
An' he 'itched 'is trousers hup a peg, an' he giv' a sort
  o' a leer.
An' he sez, 'It's werry kind, Squoire, to lighten me
  up that way ;
An' yer 've ollers been that kind to me, as before 'em
  all I 'll say.

'An' as to that same vote o' mine, 'bout which yer wish
  to know,
I never were that sort o' a man to say "Yes," mean-
  ing "No."
An' I 'll jist be free an' open, Squoire, as 'twere betwixt
  us two,
An' I 'll tell yer wot I 'm thinkin' on, an' wot I means
  to do.

'So when it comes, th' Elekshun, I ain't a goin' to fight,
A knockin' poor folk on the 'ead, an' a drinkin' till ye 're
  tight ;
An' I ain't a goin' to meetin's, where ye 're squoshed as
  flat as dough,
An' I 'll wear no ribbins in my 'at, like a Hagriculshural
  show.

'But I'll just put on my Sunday cote, an' I 'll go where
  the votes is given,
An' I 'll go there by myself, Squoire, not like a beast
  that 's driven ;
An' I woan't say nuthin' to nobody, not even my wife,
  that 's Sue ;
An' I 'll gi' my vote by ballot, Squoire, an' that 's what
  I mean to do.'

Then Mister Bull look'd orkerd, an' he star'd at the ole
    man Brown,
An' summat he said as I couldn't hear, but it cum from
    a good way down ;
An', sez he, 'Ye're larfin at me ; but my frend, I'd have
    yer know,
As it ain't the winnin' fightin-cock as fust begins to crow.'

'So, Brown,' sez he—'Nay, Squoire,' quoth he,—'As
    shure as ever is,'—
'I beg yer pardin', Squoire, I do'—'Yer'll have to pay
    for this.'
But the ole man he luk'd hinnercent, an' he softly shuk
    'is 'ead ;
'An' I means to vote by ballot,' were all the words he
    said.
    1885.

ON THE IRISH QUESTION.

THOUGHT as it all wer over, an' 'ere we're at it again,
Jus' like last long winter, wi' snow, an' slushin', an'
    rain ;
Niver no end but a muddle, an' not a word o' the cow
As they promised me last Elekshun ; ther's nun sez
    ort o' it now.

An' all for wot ? them Irish, as niver at 'ome 'ull stay,
Swarms out 'ere like rabbuts, a eatin' up poor folks
    pay ;
Wants 'Omerule they tell us. Yer stay at 'ome, sez I ;
We too 'as to live, as we'll show it yer by an' bye.

Can't make out wot it means: ther's Gladstun all for
 'em now,
As once he wer' all agen 'em, jus' like a dissolving show.
Thinks he 's gettin' too old, like Grandfather. Just *'is* way,
Cussing the yung 'uns for noise, then spilin 'em all next
 day.

Thinks he 's summat like Parson, as ollers 'as sum new
 craze,
Joos, or niggers, or Injuns, for 'oom he preaches an'
 prays;
An' shure as he sez as summat 'ull happen, you bet it fails,
'Heads,' he cries, for iver, an' th' ha'penny comes down
 'tails.'

Irish? He doan't know th' Irish; he niver worked in a
 field
'Long wi' a gang on 'em; else he 'd know, do'sn't do to
 yield
Jus' becos o' their talkin'; they'll arg' yer a hole nite long:
Wants to show a bit curridge, an' put yer foot down
 strong.

Doan't do showin' afraid: if yer ridin' a wishus mare,
Keep yer grip o' the reins, or she 'll tumble yer off sum-
 where.
Jim sez, 'Gi 'em 'Omerule!' he 's an easy fellow, is Jim:
'Get 'Omerule for yersen,' sez I—his wife rules 'im.

Wimmin is just like th' Irish. Yer let 'em open a door
Only an inch, they 'll do yer; yer 'll ne'er get shut on
 'em more:
When a should say 'keep civil,' or 'dang it'; but wot 's
 the use
Teechin' a critter like Jim, as ain't the pluck o' a goose?

Lick 'em, an' then they 'll love yer ! But bless us, an'
  'oo comes 'ere ?
Hang'd if it ain't that feller, as weedled my voat last
  year !
An' I paid for it all thro' winter. Ther 's Squoire, he
  larnt sumhow—
Lawyers can see thro' ballot—an' made a 'ell of a row.

An' then, when he wer' our Member, I ne'er got site
  o' im more ;
An' coles was, goin' at Crismas, an' none on 'em cum
  to my door ;
An' farmers cut off the milk, an' Parson, he turns 'is nose
Uppards, as I wer a midden, an' then luks down at
  'is tose.

An' wot 's the good o' losin' yer frends, as 'as been yer
  frends ?
An' tother to give yer nuthin,' but soon as Elekshun ends,
Packin' 'is carpet bag, wi' his talk an' oil on 'is tung,
Leave yer to starve ? 'Well, zur ?' 'Ole frend '—'Ole
  frend' be hung !

'Wot did yer do for me last seshun ?' 'The grand
  ole man
Sez as yer turn is comin'; he 's got the doose of a plan.
Hush ! 'twoudn't do to tell it ; if once them Tories know,
Sartin as he sez 'Yes,' Lord Randy 'ull say yer 'No';

'Only yer stick to Gladstun !' Ah, so yer sed last time,
An' didn't I stick to 'im fast, as fast as a bird in lime ?
An' a lot o' good it did me. Confound yer promises all !
Promises, nort but promise, an' th' weaker goes to the
  wall.

Now it is all them Irish,—I reads my paper, yer see,—
Parnell as gives yer trouble, so all on yer goes for he ;
An' next it 'ull be sum other, Dissenter, or God knows 'oo,
An' then yer 'll go at the Church, like 'ounds wi' a
    'ollabaloo,

Nothin' for me ! Wot say yer ? ' I'm jest a kind of
    a ass ! '
An' 'ow long wos it ago, Zur, since you too cum'd from
    grass ?
I 'm but sayin' as you did, an' Gladstun did, before ;
' Gi 'em the same as England, but niver a ha'penny
    more ! '

' Ah, but it 's trooth an' justiss ! ' That 's all very foine
    to say ;
I knows trooth an' justiss, they niver was born in a day :
It 's all lyin' an' party, an' shifts to ' Yes ' from ' No ' ;
An' confound both yer parties, as brort us to this
    'ere go !

    1886.

ON TRESPASS.

How dull the country 's gettin', I hear the nayburs
    say,
Wi' nottisses at every turn, as sez, ' No road this
    way ! '
Time wos, as one who ment no harm mite go which
    way he would,
Wi' nare a notiss in the field, or a keeper in the
    wood.

Oh, the fezzant is a skeary bird, particolarly the hen;
But I doan't see how as woods were made for fezzants
    not for men:
An' the partridg' likes a quiet field, wi' few as passes
    by;
Aye, yes, he likes to 'ave 'is way, of coorse, an' so
    do I.

We made the country wot it is, an' 'ere our 'omes 'ave
    been
Long ere he cum to set us rite, that chap in velveteen:
As, if yer walk beside a 'edge, he thinks yer 've got a
    snare,
An' yer 'at wos made for fezzant's eggs, an' yer pockit
    for a hare.

When Squoire lived 'ere I lov'd to see 'm, wi' pointer
    at 'is side;
Ther' was no drives nor battus then, as isn't sport but
    pride:
Then game was less, but sport wos more; an' he sed
    as he went by,
'Here Jim!' (that's me) 'this rabbut take, it'll feed yer
    famully.'

But now he's gone, an' summon's cum, as we 'ardly
    knows 'is name,
Sum furriner wi' frends from town, an' they say he
    sells 'is game;
Leastways he 'as a spring-cart wi' 'im, as to the town
    it goes:
An' he stays 'ere for a cupple o' weeks, an' nare a
    sowl he knows.

Now I tell yer wot, yer Gemmen, as lives in 'ouses
 grand,
Yer 've got the luck, yer 've got the gould, an' ye 're
 owners o' the land;
But the countryside wer made for all; God made it
 open, free,
An' 'twer niver ment to be shut up, like door wi' lock
 an' key.

An' I 'ate to walk on pathways, an' I 'ate to live by
 rool,
'Yer must, yer musn't, go that road,' jus' like a child
 at school;
An' I 'ate to see the old ways stopp'd, wher' ollers
 ways 'ave been;
An', formost-fust, I 'ate 'im wust, that chap in velveteen.

But I likes to 'ave things plezzant, an' I grudges nun
 'is sport;
An' I likes the good old famullies, as wos o' the rite
 old sort;
As shot, an' fished, an' hunted fair, for the plezzure,
 not the game,
An' loved the old place wher' they lived, an' knew us
 all by name.

But these new folk as ties things up is another biz-
 ness quite;
An' a country ain't worth livin' in wher' trespass is
 too tite :
An' if the law's agen the poor, an' for them as 'as the tin,
Well, I 've a voat, an' if they fight, we'll see 'oose side
 'ull win.

 1887.

THE JEWBILLEE.

WE lives in a biggish villidge, sum calls it a smallish town,
An' we thinks ourselves good Churchmen, an' we're all
　　for Queen an' Crown :
An' Parson, he likes things stirrin', so he up an' he
　　sez, sez he,
' It's time as we 'ad a meetin', to tork o' this Jewbillee.'

So the meetin' it cum together, an' Parson, he tuk the
　　chair,
An' sez he, ' Dear frends, th' occashun is won hun-
　　commonly rare ;
An' the owld Church wants a pulpit, an' summut to
　　last, yer see,
Is the thing as yer should be seekin', 'bove all at a
　　Jewbillee.'

Then arter 'im spoke our Plumber, we calls 'im
　　Crotchetty Crump,
(An' he 'ummed an' he 'awed amazin'), ' Wot say yer
　　to 'avin' a pump,
Wi' the Royal Harms hemblazoned, an' hopen to all
　　an' free,
An' that 'ull be summut lastin' to tell of our Jewbillee ? '

Then next to 'im rose our Brewer, who sed wi' a
　　cunnin' leer,
' Yer pump be hanged ! Let's gi' em a spred, wi' plenty
　　o' beer :
An' ther's some as 'ull 'ave 'ot coppers a takin' ther
　　glass too free,
An' tha't ull be fine an' lastin' to 'mind 'em of Jewbillee.'

An' the therd on 'em wer' the Grocer, 'oose name it
    is Dodger Mills,
An' ther's nothin' as he won't sell yer, from pepper-
    mint up to pills;
An' sez he, ' Yer beer's all pison ; let's gi' 'em a hole-
    some tea,
Wi' sugar at will : doan't stint 'em, my frends, at a
    Jewbillee ! '

Then I 'erd as it wer' a snortin' fro' won as beside me
    sat,—
Our Butcher—he spoke it sittin', becos he wer' short
    an' fat—
An', ' Tea's very well for wimmen ; but beef for men,'
    sez he,
' Wi' plenty o' suet pudden's the thing for a Jewbillee.'

And Milkman, he bragg'd 'is butter, an' Baker, he puff'd
    'is bred :
An' Parson, he tried to stop 'em, but they wasn't at
    Church, they sed :
An' I thort as they'd all get fightin', for non' on 'em
    could agree,
But each on 'em 'ad 'is 'obby to ride for the Jewbillee.

Sez Brewer, ' Yer sand yer shugar': sez Grocer,
    ' That same's a lie':
' If ye say that again,' says Brewer, ' take care or I'll
    black yer eye'
(Jus' like one of them wild Irish in Parlerment all so
    free),
' An' that 'ull be summut lastin' to show for yer Jew-
    billee.'

Then sudden I 'erd a snortin' agen, an' it 's my belief
As Butcher'd 'ave gon for summun, unless they had
    gon for beef :
So savidge he turn'd on Grocer wi' a word as begins
    wi' D,
Which I'm shure I will never repeat it, leastways at a
    Jewbillee.

But at last they 'ave made things plezzant by takin' 'em
    all in a lump,
Pulpit, an' beer, an' pudden', an' beef, an' a tea, an'
    pump :
An' the men is to 'ave a dinner, an' the young an' the
    old a tea,
An' that 's 'ow we got it settled down 'ere for the
    Jewbillee.

P.S.

The dinner 's for folk not sixty, an' I wer' sixty in
    May :
So I take 's my famully Bible, an' halters the month an'
    day :
An' if this hain't quite propper, why a loyal feller like
    me,
He shure-ly shouldn't be habsent, left hout of a Jewbillee.

    1887.

PENULTIMATE.

Sitting with a vacant brow
    In a chimney-corner cold ;
Winter, always winter. now,
    See him ageing ! Hodge is old.

Cottage stripped from floor to roof,
  Cupboard empty, larder bare!
Hunger hardly kept aloof,
  Oh, how hard, by parish care!

While the hand whose mighty clutch
  Tore the oak up, giant-strong,
Barely can sustain a crutch,
  Barely lift the lame along:

And the hour foreseen afar
  Comes with sickness, ache, and pain;
Stricken by an evil star,
  Fallen, he cannot rise again.

Bit by bit 'twas gathered in,
  Bit by bit his treasure flies,
Till with nothing but his skin,
  All is over, and he dies.

Then—Nay, leave him there alone!
  Fare-thee-well, Hodge, honest fellow!
Something still is to be done
  Nature's crab in thee to mellow:

Shape thy life on loftier plan,
  Give it aim, and hope, and relish,
Leave thee still unvarnished man,
  Yet with art thy lot embellish:

Keep thee sober, saving, healthy,
  Merrier as in days of old;
With enough to live on, wealthy,
  Leaving us the race for gold:

Perhaps a cottage all thine own,
   Ready money for thy baker,
Butcher's meat not quite unknown,
   And (perchance) 'the cow and acre.' *a*

Who will do this, he shall be
   ' *Civitatis dux et pater,*'
Leader, chief, at least to me,
   And—confound the Agitator!

FINIS.

THE old man is dead; lay him low!
White as snow was his head; lay him low!
Lay him low in the earth where he laboured so long,
While his arm it was lusty, his heart it was strong,
      Long ago:
There were men in our hamlet both comely and tall,
But he was the leader, the stoutest of all:
   Ah, how brief is our life! Lay him low!

Who are these that escort to the grave?
Mourners meet for the true and the brave?
   Oh! he worked for us well!
Surely beauty will weep, wealth and honour will
   come,
For the soldier of industry borne to his tomb:
      Tongues will tell,
How he bore sun and frost, snow and storm, for our
   sake;
Nothing seemed his great strength, his high courage
   to shake,
   Till at last in our service he fell.

Who are these then, his cortège of woe?
Wife, and child? Nay, they died long ago.
Friends, and neighbours? A pauper's? Ah, no!
          Look and see!
Note it well! Three old shadows, three paupers, are
     all
Who limp after—the parish finds coffin and pall—
While the Autumn-winds rave, and the Autumn-leaves
     fall: .
          Only three!
Three old shadows! And one, by his horrible glee,
Has been drinking. In drink the crushed spirit goes
     free:
     He forgets that he still is a thrall. β

Yet his work! Oh, but think! Fen and field
From their wildness redeemed, till they yield
Fruit and grain! And the swamp-fever healed
     By the sweat of his brow!
As he moved on his way, 'neath his masterful tread
Some plague was uprooted, some ague-fit fled;
Earth blossomed beneath him, sky brightened o'erhead;
     Where the thistle grew rank, harvests grow.

Best of conquerors! Peace has its crown
Well as war. Though no marble look down
On his bones; yet above him the sod will be green,
And on high where more truly true service is seen,
     He too shall not lack his renown.

But his faults! Nay, we know them. His lot
Was a hard one. Now all be forgot!
All but this, that as long as he could he worked on:

Q

How he suffered, none knew: even now he is gone,
We scarce guess how he bore his sad burden alone.
      Wet or dry,
Hot or cold, he complained not; took things as they
    came;
Bad luck! wretched cards! still he played out the
    game;

Semi-blind, racked with gravel, rheumaticky, lame,
Groaning inward, yet cheery, still outward the same!
    Then hushed be the world's jest, and moist be the
    eye!
      Hats off, as the coffin goes by!

ᴜ. p. 224. A Scotch farmer suggests as an alternative—' With
a goat and half-an-acre,' adding, ' the milk is verra gude, and the
beast will eat anything; but she's a deevil to climb.'

β. p. 225. An incident, like that here described, is said, in
Lord Shaftesbury's life, to have given him the first impulse to
his labours for the poor. Things are better now.

THE END.

www.ingramcontent.com/pod-product-compliance
Lightning Source LLC
Chambersburg PA
CBHW030821020726
47499CB00006B/2017